Following fate or the lines of life

in the palm of my hand?

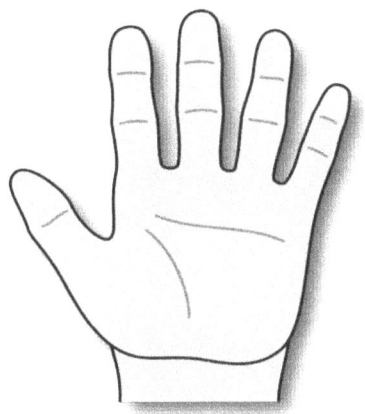

Lifelines

Peggy Kohlmeyer

Edited Print

ISBN-13-978: 0692743638

ISBN-10-0692743634

Library of Congress Control Number: **XXXXX (If applicable)**

My story is dedicated to:

My dad, who I will always admire,

My husband Mike, who is my best friend and hero,

And Susanne, whose friendship I will always appreciate and value forever.

Some of the characters in this book are fictional.

Some are based on real people and events that positively influenced my life.

To those who are mentioned, I humbly extend my gratitude to you for the encouraging influence you had on me.

"You look fine."

Individuals who have experienced brain injuries often hear this. Brain injury is a hidden issue that causes frustration, pain, and oftentimes a lack of understanding because from the outside, many who have experienced a brain injury "look fine."

Contents

Chapter 1
On Any Given Monday

For it being a Monday morning, Ed Hayes didn't think he'd ever been so excited to see another one. Mondays are the days that most everyone else has to go back to work. He'd lost count of his Mondays. Three months is a long time. He's done now, and it is summer and June. Getting out of jail this Monday morning. It' been a long three-month stint.

Jail time was a lot harder for Ed this time. He actually had time to sober up. He's sober, though, and now ready to leave. He's served his time. This marks his third release, since it was his third arrest for driving while intoxicated, or DWI. The first one was a fender bender, only damaging his car, while the second didn't even involve anyone else, with him failing a sobriety checkpoint test.

This DWI was different. This time the driver was a girl, and he hit her car from the side and broke her leg. Sure, he'd lost his driver's license and his job and served his third incarceration, but actually, it really didn't matter to him. It only added to his drunk-driving record, earning more points against him on his license.

Walking out of the jail, putting himself into a positive state of mind, Ed Hayes reminded himself, "It's a great day," if only for his own satisfaction. I mean, he is getting out of jail. And a three-month incarceration did give him time to sit and think. With all the time that he had in the facility to think, he would've rather the opposite had happened, and he'd gotten the broken leg himself. If he'd gotten the broken leg instead of the girl, he could've still been out and gotten drunk. For him it would've been a double benefit: paid time off from his job while not having to sober up. Thinking the better of a bad situation, he's sure he made an even trade. Ed did the crime, so he did the tim**e.**

Reminding himself that he's a reformed man, getting into the car, he gives his wife that token hello kiss with a peck on her check. "Darling, I'm a new man," sharing his positive attitude if only as a charade. He's also fortunate that she agreed to pick him up. As it's Monday, his wife is in a hurry to make her shift at work. After thirty years of marriage, you'd think she'd have a clue of what's important to him. Thinking in jail by himself, he did miss her each and every time, his best friend, alcohol.

Ed knows that each drink for him it's only for the intoxication with every sip. Yes, in every drink, he can get a little more buzzed, and a little more drunk. Again, a three-month incarceration gave him time to sit and think. He can't handle the consequences of spending any more time in jail, since he also can't handle going that long without a drink. If it's a beer, liquor, or even in a situation of desperation, a glass of wine. It's simple; it's all for the taste of alcohol. He'll take the consequences, whatever they are. He just can't let his wife know what he has to do.

Back at their house, turning off the TV, feeling enough time for hellos has passed, he squawks to his wife, "I'm gonna go check out what I've missed at the dealership." He's saying he's on his way to see what's happened at the Ford dealership where he used to work, but it's an excuse to pick up his usual morning routine with a pit stop at the liquor store, which is only for a quick one. He'll consider a stop at this store as the first step in his own recovery plan. Ed concludes with, "Good-bye, honey!" Content with his decision, quietly closing their front door behind him, letting out his breath.

With the beer that he buys, he slips on the can cover that's in the car. This keeps his drink hidden from others and conceals the evidence that he's a drinking man. Hearing the *pop* at the top of the can and the escape of the *whoosh*, Ed's feeling that this one is going to be even better than his first. His mouth is in a state of anxiety waiting for that simple swig. Gulping it almost in desperation, he sputters while coughing out the words of his warm greeting, "Darlin', how good to see you again." Not like he's cheating on his wife; it's only a cool beer in his hand.

Getting to the Ford auto dealership on his first free morning, he wants to share his hellos with the guys where he used to work. Showing his face, he's proof that prison didn't beat him down. Ed feels that he's got to prove that prison didn't take him this time, nope, not this time. Also, what can they say? They know that he'll always have a friend, another close friend, but this time he's already moved on to the one named Jim. His friend Jim Beam, that is, or Old Crow, whichever price is good in a brown paper bag disguising the evidence that he's got at 11:00 a.m. Anyway, he's only visiting the premises, saying hi, since he needs a place to hang out until the Night Owl Lounge opens at 1:00 p.m. and continues as he drinks and sits.

11:00 a.m. to 12:00 p.m. and finally 1:00 p.m., two hours and time to leave. No, not that he's already tired of them, but he can tell that they're getting tired of him, hanging around, almost becoming an eyesore. Also, he's got to go find another friend with the empty bottle now in his hand. Anyway, it's after 12:00 p.m. in a college town, and some of the bars are starting to open, with him having a good buzz going on.

The Night Owl Lounge is convenient from the dealership, Ed reminds himself. It's less than a mile drive across the median, on the left-hand side up the Atlanta highway. Hopefully, he'll only blend in. Three months is a long time, and he wonders if anyone has missed him. Will Tami, the fancy red-haired waitress, still be there? Will the owner let him keep another credit tab? He'll have to ask early, since he doesn't have much cash.

"Welcome back," erupts as he opens the Night Owl's front door. Walking up, the owner greets him with his extended hand, asking quickly, "Where have you been, man? Hayes, where have you been?"

"I had to do some time. Some time that was my mistake, but it won't happen again," drinking earlier today on an empty stomach. Now feeling queasy, he quickly sits in his signature spot. "But let me have a cold one with that burger and fries."

One o'clock p.m., then two, then four, followed by eight o'clock p.m. He knows he's been drinking, drinking a lot, and he needs to get home. Tomorrow is the start to another day, and tomorrow he needs to get serious and get a job. Where would he get a job this time? Serious thoughts, though, that he doesn't want to think about. Even more important for him right now is that he wants another drink. "Yeah, Teresa, just add it to my bill."

As a mechanic at the local Ford dealership, he had it perfect. He'd work from eight until five, stop here after work until eight or nine, and be home by ten. This gave him time to sober up and make it back to work the next morning. Him drunk on the job? What, him? Yes, he had gotten a few warnings, but then he learned what he thought was a brilliant disguise. If he didn't shave for a few days, he'd just look rough all the time.

Liquor, always his only friend, Teresa adds another one to his bill and as he reminds himself that'll be his last one. He has to drive. He's good until he gets out to the parking lot. Ed only has to put the lock in the key, nope, that's not it, put the car key in the lock. He has it, he has it, and he knows he has it. "I'll say three tries is a charm."

Getting his car key in the lock, he questions why he even bothered to lock this piece of shit car. A Ford Thunderbird is not his choice to drive, but it's heavy, and it runs. He has to watch out because it's his hands that swerve, and that makes the car swerve. Isn't that the reason he'd gotten his three DWIs?

He reminds himself of the guidelines for getting back home. First, pull out of the parking lot, and turn the left onto the Atlanta Highway. Next, keep his hands locked on the steering wheel to make the three-mile drive home, passing the Georgia Square Mall.

On the same Monday, two miles up the road. It's 9:00 p.m., and Casual Corner at the Georgia Square Mall is preparing to close for the day. Glancing at the posted employee schedule, I have to make sure I'm off on Friday. Mom's

coming home, and I've got to drive to Atlanta to

pick her up. Also confirming that I'm scheduled

to work again the next day, mentally I grin. You

know, the kind where you're smiling on the inside

because if people saw you smiling on the outside,

you'd have to explain something that they might

not understand. How would I explain that even

though it's summer and even though there's more

exciting things to do outside the mall, I'm smiling

because I get to work again? Before signing out

for the night, I only have to straighten up the

fitting room.

Finally calling it a night, Brenda, the store

manager, and I step out of the store and into the

mall. As she turns back to lock the door: "Thanks

again for filling in for Olivia tonight, Peggy." Heart-

fully replying, I remind her, "Hey, it's worth it,"

while reflecting on Julie's smiles from the outfits I created and coordinated for her. Adding while I have her attention, "Oh, I'll see you tomorrow at my normal time," reminding her that I checked the schedule. Without saying much of anything else, we both make our way out to the front glass entrance of the mall. When we set off the sensors the automatic sliding glass doors *swoosh* open. This hot Athens air feels like the sauna some girls pay for. Yes, it's summer, and I'm still a student, but I remind myself that this is my last semester at Georgia. My smile this time is evident as it spreads across my face. It's not that this feeling is totally new to me, but I'm just one more day closer to achieving my goal of earning my degree and gaining my full independence.

As I step off the concrete sidewalk and onto the asphalt of the mall parking lot, my attention is redirected to the summer heat. It's now a little after nine, with the mall closing for the night and the heat of the day still radiating. Coming from the air conditioner in the mall and wanting the air conditioner in my car, I quickly find my gray Mazda in the mall parking lot. Glancing up, I see the brightness of the summer night sky. Staring up at the stars while they stare back at me, I remember the childhood rhyme: S*tar light, star bright, the first star I see tonight, I wish I may, I wish I might…* So is this my time to make that wish? My wish? Like maybe wondering and wishing what's going to happen to me next? Catching myself deep in thought, how do I wish for something that I already know? Something that I've already planned to take place? I know that after this summer of classes, I'm fulfilling an internship in Columbus, Georgia. That'll complete my degree. But then what's next? Do I make the transition into adulthood by moving back into my father's home first and then looking for an apartment? Even more, if I fulfill my internship, is there an opportunity for me to get a permanent position afterward? But if I stay in Columbus, am I settling for something less? This is only followed by my thought that if I have my own apartment, it will fully mark my independence, completely living on my own. I'm really thinking, what is next for me? I have too many questions about my future to ponder, and totally forget about seeing a star or even making a silly wish as I focus back on starting my car and seeing Mom when she comes back to the United States.

Navigating out of the mall parking lot, there's a long line of cars at the traffic light, waiting to turn onto the Atlanta Highway. Having to wait and therefore having more time to think ahead, which I always do. Julie should beat me back home since she's had the day off. Like me, she's got a retail job at the mall. Our only difference is our work locations. She's at the Champ's Sporting Goods store on the upper level, while Casual Corner, where I work, is on the lower level. Champ's dress code calls for athletic wear, and therefore, her personal wardrobe is totally different. Her visit to the store tonight was such a surprise, and I thanked her for boosting my sales.

As I leave the mall, everyone is out, wanting to get somewhere else, even if it is just going home. As I think other thoughts, traffic time passes, as I finally make it through the green light and make the left turn onto the Atlanta Highway. I'll try to remind myself to thank Olivia for asking me to work for her. I mean, it's been such a great night! What if I had only stayed at home?

Chapter 2
Bernstein's Funeral Home

Hearing the crash outside, louder than the thunder from a storm, Sam and Jason walk closer to the two cars, Sam's stomach turning at what he sees.   "Oh my gosh, oh my gosh, stay where you are, medic is on the way." Talking to the girl. "Jason, you call nine-one-one, and I'll go to the other side and see if anyone else is still alive."

"This is nine-one-one. What's your emergency?"

"There's been an accident, a bad one, right out front."

"Sir, where are you?"

"Ah...oh, Bernstein's Funeral Home on the Atlanta Highway."

"Sir, what can you tell me about the accident?"

"Well, it's two cars, and one is a small, kinda like compact car…I saw it when I first went out there. I'm thinking it's a Mazda. It's going up the right way of the highway like it's supposed to, but the other one is a larger, darker car, a Thunderbird, and it's going the wrong way. That Thunderbird hit the Mazda head on. I mean, that Thunderbird didn't cross to its side, you know, over the median. They hit right out in front, I mean, right at the top of the hill. Right out in front of the funeral home. Man, the crash was so loud, Jason and I heard it from inside."

"Sir, could you tell how many people were involved?"

"Well, two, I mean, I think there was one in each car. I think it's a girl in the Mazda. I couldn't really see…Sam went out to go check. The other one has to be a guy. It looks like he's already trying to get out of his car."

"Sir, tell me what you can see of their injuries."

"Nothing seems to be wrong with the man, but the girl, gosh, I can't see her body, and the engine of her car is smashed back, to like where she's supposed to be."

"Sir, thank you for your call. Medic and police are on their way."

"Yes, officer, the crash was so loud Jason and I heard it from inside," Sam responds, standing with his back toward the accident, facing the police officer, unable to look at the Mazda again. "Checking things out, I called out to the girl, and it's as if I was talking to no one. I mean, she didn't seem to hear me. I mean, it's like I was talking to no one…almost like she was…like, dead. I mean, I looked at her face….and it's like it's all smashed up. I mean look at her." Sam points behind him, making sure to keep eye contact with the Athens officer, not able to turn to look at her again. "I couldn't handle it, and then y'all show up. I mean, what's an old guy on a Monday night doing driving if he's that drunk? Didn't he know that he was on the wrong side of the road?"

"Yes, officer, we both heard it," Jason shares, joining the activity outside. "After I called nine-one-one and came out with Sam, that guy in the Thunderbird, he rolls out, falls out all over the street. He couldn't even lift himself up. I went over to help him up. And he just reeked of alcohol. I mean, can't you smell it? Officer, he just stinks."

Jason pointed to the front of the guy's car. "Was he just so drunk that he didn't even turn his headlights on?"

"Coming up that hill, he couldn't see her car, and then without his headlights," the Athens' police officer shares with the guys, as if in confirmation.

"What's going to happen to him? I mean, just look at him. He can't even stand up he's so drunk. Do you think that gash on his forehead means anything?"

"Guys, thanks for your call and support. The EMTs are transferring the girl to Saint Mary's Hospital. The gentleman will be placed under arrest and checked for any injuries."

Refocusing back to the girl, "Does she have a chance?" Sam and Jason query, almost in unison.

"Do you think that girl is going to live?" Jason asks again, as a closing thought.

On the phone in another city, an hour or so later, the voice says, "Yes, I'm calling from the

Saint Mary's emergency room, and I need to speak with a Dr. Pike."

"This is Dr. Pike, Ben Pike."

"I'm calling in reference to an accident that's happened. We have a patient in the intensive care unit of our emergency room. Your number was found in her car."

"What? An accident? One of my girls has been in a car accident?"

"Sorry, but yes, sir. A person with the driver's license identification as Peggy Pike is at Saint Mary's Hospital in intensive care. Yes, she's been in an accident. Your phone number was in her wallet as an emergency contact. This *is an emergency*. You're needed at Saint Mary's for proper identification of the individual mentioned. If it is her, your signature is needed to proceed."

"Oh god, how bad is it? What's she like—? I mean, I'll be right there."

Back to Athens. "Katie? This is your dad. Your sister's been in a car accident."

"What? Oh hey, Daddy. What do you mean, a car accident?"

"Someone from the Saint Mary's emergency room just called me. He said I needed to come to the hospital."

"Daddy, how did they know to call you? I mean, I'm here in Athens and closer; shouldn't they have called me first?"

"He said something about my phone number in her car or in her purse. Along with her driver's license. Katie, you'll just have to pick me up at the airport."

"Shouldn't I go to the hospital first? I mean, how long is it going to take you?"

"No. I mean, I thought of that, but by the time you go to the hospital, I'll be at the airport waiting for you. Just come pick me up, and we'll go together. We need to hurry. They say she's in critical condition."

"OK, Dad. I'm on my way."

As my life hangs by a thread, again I briefly wonder what if I had stayed home tonight.

Chapter 3
Hope Avenue

Hope Avenue is the perfect name for the perfect street for the perfect family to live and grow up, but we aren't that perfect family…yet. Hope Avenue is in the Five Points area of Athens. Nope, not the Athens in Greece nor Athens, Ohio, but the Athens in Georgia. Athens is where Mom and Daddy met while they were both attending the University of Georgia, or UGA. Daddy came from the small town of Mauk, Georgia, which is fourteen miles from Buena Vista, Georgia (with the correct southern pronunciation as *Bue-naw Vista*), while Mom drove from the Athens neighborhood of Glenwood, maybe four miles away from the UGA campus.

In Athens, Georgia, at Five Points, a newly single mom with two kids is something this

conservative community isn't yet ready to accept.
With us moving to Hope Avenue, I'm taking this as
a positive message for my family. I mean, Mom is
trying, but what can you say to a divorced mom
with two kids, both under the age of three. Why
Hope Avenue? With our move back to Athens
without our dad, on this street with its name, for me
it means that that's all that's left: Hope. It's only a
single street connecting South Lumpkin to Milledge
Terrace, and it's only the people who live here that
want to come here. Even more, Milledge Terrace is
no thoroughfare to anywhere else, since it dead ends
to a home-labeled Sleepy Hollow. This is what
Mom now needs, though, the stability of a safe but
dull and sleepy neighborhood and Hope.

My mom's mom, whom we call Mimi, and
my mom's dad, Poder, together make up my
grandparents in Athens. They are the connection or

reason to bring us here, back to Athens and Hope Avenue. It's almost like Mom's moves have been in a full circle, and this is how it all started…from what I know.

Katie and I are only fourteen months apart in age. Katie was born on November 5, while my birthdate is January 1. My birth also marks the year that Daddy is graduating from medical school, and I don't think I'm the graduation present he really wanted. Heck, I couldn't even make it quick enough to be born one day earlier in December, to give Mom and Daddy the dependent child care tax break for the previous year. Instead, I had to hold out and wait until the next day, or New Years of the following year. Giving credit to Mom, though, she never lets me think I'm a mistake. She reminds me that I might not have been planned for, but everyone in the world celebrates my birthday.

Following her kind statement, I remind her that it's December 31, or New Year's Eve, that people celebrate. It's my *birth* day that they might start their new year's resolutions with regrets, having to recover from their hangovers and celebration from the night before.

With our move to Athens and Mom coming back home, I'm eighteen months old and Katie my sister is already thirty-two months old, or a little over two and a half. This means that no matter how hard I try, Katie's without a doubt is always going to be fourteen months ahead of me. Of course, since she's older, she'll always be ahead of me in age, so that also puts her ahead of me in school, but with her blond hair and big, bold, brown eyes she is also ahead of me in looks. She's my sibling whom I'll always admire and envy. Attempting to give me equal attention and flattery, Mom steps in, referring to me as her beautiful brunette. Realizing her efforts, I only have to look in the mirror, and I see what others see, that there's nothing exciting about me. It's brown hair, mousy brown hair at that, which only allows some dullness to shine, and with a pug nose that turns up at the end.

Looking at our living situation, overall you can say Mom has really gotten screwed. I mean, Mom put her degree and her life on hold to help Daddy with his degree and career. Originally, she even moved away from her family for him. Now she's back but with no degree, no husband and two kids or, more nicely, the wrong end of the deal. Yes, children are a blessing, but let's ask you to trade places with anyone in Mom's situation. Then you'll know how strapped she feels.

Katie and I are told that Daddy left without any explanation. Or rather, no explanation to us, but what do you explain to a child at my age? I mean, I'm not even making complete sentences when I decide to blabber or talk, and at a little over two and a half, Katie is still making attempts to go potty solo. So what can we know or even understand?

Daddy? We don't even know that he's missing, and we think that his absence is the normal way for all families. We're reminded of him by what's stated in their divorce agreement. Mom has to make sure that we talk to him on every holiday and birthday, and Daddy has to make sure he takes us in the summer. He's just not around anymore, not even in family pictures. Fortunately, Poder, my mom's dad, does step in every now and then, and for our dad, how can you miss someone who isn't there?

Katie and I are going to preschool at our church, Saint James United Methodist on the corner of West Lake Drive and South Lumpkin. Our church is one block from our house on Hope Avenue and just a shout from Mimi and Poder's house on Glenwood Drive.

During the week, Mom drops us off at preschool in the morning with hugs, kisses, and good wishes for the day. But before noon Mimi picks us up to eat lunch with her. Sometimes we get to take our nap and spend the rest of the afternoon with her, too. Also, with Mimi helping to watch after us, Mom is going back to school to take that additional step that is expected of her and earn her master's degree.

Living on Hope Avenue seems a great convenience to everything. We're only a block from the church and less than a two-mile drive from Mimi and Poder's house or that shouting distance from the church. In the opposite direction, we're about three blocks from Five Points.

Five Points? This is the area named for the intersection of Milledge Circle, Lumpkin Street, and Milledge Avenue. These three streets all come to one center traffic light, thus marking it Five Points. This area caters to the college crowd. Sandwich shops are on either side, along with a Sons of Italy pizza place additionally lined up with some boutiques. At Five Points, you'll also find groceries at Bell's, with prescriptions and sundries at Hodgson's Pharmacy, followed by the Five Points Dry Cleaner and a gas station with a convenience store called Handy Andy. For a kid like me, this constitutes a hub of activity. Five Points is my town.

Chapter 4
First Grade

Katie's been at Barrow Elementary for two years, and she's pretty comfortable starting her third-grade year. Me? I'm finally making it to the first grade. I'm a little scared since everything is new to me. I mean, even starting our day. Instead of taking a left turn at the end of our street to get to Saint James, we are now having to take a right turn from Hope Avenue to get to Barrow Elementary School. Instead of us having the opportunity to walk to our preschool at the church, Mom gets up extra early to drive us to school every morning. This seems to make the day that much longer, driving through the Five Points traffic light and sitting in our car until the traffic light turns red.

So far, my first day is fantastic. After Mom and I walk Katie to her third-grade class, I get solo time with Mom as she walks me to my first-grade class. Lifting my chin up and straightening my hair, Mom gives me a kiss on the check. As if she's loaning me over for the day, she says, "Peg, you're set. Your first day of school. You're growing up so fast!" She introduces herself to Mrs. Aldridge, my first-grade teacher, before leaving and going to her own school.

Of course, by now we're supposed to know our numbers, letters, and colors. Whew! Thank goodness I don't have to worry about any of this. I learned all of those when Katie was with me at Saint James preschool, and I actually started reading real words after she left. For our first assignment to check all this out, Mrs. Aldridge gives each of her

first-grade students a huge, I mean huge, piece of
white paper.

I'm already glowing with the opportunity to
demonstrate my educational foundations, but my
curiosity is now up. How am I going to do this?
This paper is so big that it's bigger than each of us
in this class. Thankfully, with this paper Mrs.
Aldridge instructs us about our elbow buddy. She
tells us to "Look to the student sitting next to you at
your table, at your elbow." This is our classmate or
partner we are paired up with at the table to work.
Mrs. Aldridge gives us our assignment of having
them make our silhouettes. She guides us: "As one
of the partners lays down on the paper, the elbow
buddy or the other student you were sitting next to
at your table draws a solid line, making a silhouette
around the other student's body." Oh, so we're only
drawing each other. I can do that!

Peggy Kohlmeyer

Missy is on the right of my elbow, and I am on the left of her elbow. Since we're the only two people at our table, we're the only match. We laugh as I tell her that I am right handed, and she tells me she is left handed. Right now, we both know that we're going to be best friends. It's already set, since we're a perfect match, sharing a nervous laugh for our first assignment and something as simple as sketching the other's silhouette.

For more room, Mrs. Aldridge sends our class outside to the front of the school where the sidewalk goes in both ways. Missy's waving me over, having grabbed a spot of the sidewalk in the shade. Laughing, I have to tell her, "Missy, you're acting like Flat Stanley from the book."

"Who's that?" she asks, as I begin to draw her silhouette for our first assignment. Not believing that everyone doesn't know about *Flat*

Stanley, I tell her, "I'll bring you my book tomorrow. It's my favorite book. I mean, my utmost favorite of all books, so I can let you read it for the day, but since it's my favorite, I'll have to take it back home." Thinking to myself as I swallow the promise I've just made. Share my utmost favorite book? Boy, I hope she's really going to be my best friend.

As I am continuing my pencil line to reach to the side of her head, Missy is nodding it in agreement, realizing the message of friendship that I've just made. Telling her, "Hold still. You're going to make me draw your head too big," as we both giggle, making the connection of how smart we both are as first graders.

I draw around her body, ending back at her arm. Missy sits up. Standing up beside her drawing, we both see how well I've done. "I wish the

Peggy Kohlmeyer

sidewalk were smoother." Pointing to the ripples of the pencil marks. Wanting my first assignment to have perfection and silently challenging Missy to draw better than me.

Now it's my turn. I lay flat, also like Stanley from the book, and Missy draws around my shape. When she's finished drawing me and I'm standing up, we both step back and look at our drawings and silently compare. Yes, her lines of me are bumpy, too, but in her drawing of me, I don't like what I see. I'm just plain fat.

In my drawing of Missy, she's just so thin and small. I didn't think this was possible. When we each got such a big piece of paper, I couldn't even carry it without crinkling it up, but now my body just hogs the entire page. Asking myself did Missy do this on purpose, or am I really just that big? When a picture speaks a thousand words, I don't like what I see.

Missy, standing next to me, is also looking at what we have drawn. She doesn't say anything either about me being so much bigger than her, as if it doesn't register. Instead she says, "Your lines are so straight and solid around my body, but look at mine. They seem to be more like squiggle marks." Fortunately, her comment interrupts my thinking and brings me back to our assignment. Next? For each student to write what we want to be when we grow up.

For this task, I don't even have to think. I'm ready to write what I want to do when I get to be an adult like Mom. I want to teach. Even more, I want to draw Poder instead of me. He's the best teacher ever. I mean, he's even higher than a teacher; he's a professor right now. Poder teaches every day when he drives to the university. He gets to go home for lunch, and every day Mimi makes sure to have him a sandwich ready. After his lunch, when his teaching schedule is right, Poder also gets to take a nap. He's who I want to be like. Yes, I want to teach. It's Poder I've decided I'll have to draw.

Glancing to my side, I see Missy has taken my idea. She's drawn a girl with pigtails with an apple in her left hand and a ruler in her right hand. Missy strongly states, "My mom is a kindergarten teacher right now, and my daddy is a football teacher. That's what they do, so I'll have to do that, too."

So, Missy's mom is like the ladies at Saint James preschool. You mean they were my teachers? Sure, I learned my letters, numbers, and colors, but mostly I remember their fuss getting out our bedrolls for nap time and making sure the red Kool-Aid didn't get on anyone's clothes. That's what her mom does? That's it. Missy is using my idea.

Thinking and thinking, trying to figure out what I'm going to draw, now I'm completely lost. Nope, not a doctor; that's what Daddy does, and look where it got Mom. Not a veterinarian, because that's what Katie said she wanted to be yesterday, and I'll never copy her.

Then it hits me. A ballerina! I've got my first ballet class after school today, and no one else is using the color pink. After drawing the ballerina with her tutu and ribbons around the ballet shoes, I draw a smile on my face.

The next day at school, as I promised, I share my *Flat Stanley* book with Missy. We take turns reading it. One page for her, the following page for me. When we're finished reading, we're laughing so hard about how much fun it'll be to be a

Flat Stanley. No, not to be flattened out by the heavy bulletin board after it falls on you, but to fly like a kite or go through the mail and visit her grandparents like a letter. Why would she want to go through the mail like a letter? Quickly, I try to explain to her that I only see my dad in the summer for a month. Yes, I guess it's hard, but what else do I know? Escalating with hope, I tell her I don't care so much about the kite, with Mimi and Poder living in town, but if I'm a letter, I'd get to visit my dad. He could even put "Return to Sender" and send me back home if my visit wasn't at the right time. I can tell Missy isn't sure what to say to me or how to respond, still having both parents. "It's OK," is all that I hear from her as she gives me back my favorite book.

After we finish my book, before school really begins, when the 8:30 a.m. school bell rings,

Mrs. Aldridge and Ms. Hicks call Missy and me out of Mrs. Aldridge's class into the hallway. Looking up at the hallway wall, our silhouette drawings from yesterday's assignment are hanging for everyone to see. Ms. Hicks asks, "Girls, will each of you read what you've written on your posters?"

Looking at our pictures, with me reading first since she is pointing to my ballerina up on the wall, I smile as I say, "When I grow up, I want to be a ballerina." Since I had my first ballet class yesterday after school, I know that I'm already working toward achieving this goal. "I want to dance to the music as it plays. I want to perform in front of people. I want to dance into people's hearts." Ms. Hicks and Mrs. Aldridge talk small to each other. Looking at Missy, I wonder if she can hear them. Glancing at me and looking nervous, her eyes say no.

Peggy Kohlmeyer

It's Missy's turn next. At the bottom of her

picture with her as the teacher she reads, "I want to

be a teacher when I grow up. I want to teach the

letters and numbers. I want to teach children to read.

I want children to read to me." As Missy takes her

turn and reads her passage, I begin to clench my fist,

since I feel that she's taken my idea away from me.

Clenching my fists tighter and tighter as she gets to

her end, my hands begin to hurt as my fingernails go

into each of my palms, since secretly I know that's

me. No, not just to teach students to read but to

write and for each of my students to share their

thoughts about what they have also written.

I look at Ms. Hicks and Mrs. Aldridge. They

are talking small again to each other almost as if to

whisper, while seeming to agree as I hear,

"Passages are so well written and expressed for the

first grade." I am still holding my *Flat Stanley*

book. Ms. Hicks asks, "Peggy open your book and pick a page for Missy to read." Which I do.

Knowing my book, I give it to Missy, and it's turned to my favorite page. It's the part at the end when Flat Stanley is tired of being Flat, and even though he has had fun, he just wants to be normal Stanley again. As Missy reads this paragraph from the book, I finish it up with her, since the words are in my head. I mean, it is my favorite book. Again, Ms. Hicks is impressed and Mrs. Aldridge agrees, too.

"Girls, you are going to move to Ms. Hicks's class," are the words that I hear Mrs. Aldridge share. "Oh" is all that I say. Thinking of leaving Mrs. Aldridge's class with the big wooden tables and going to Ms. Hicks's class, where each student has their own desks.

Peggy Kohlmeyer

"Oh" is only what I hear Missy say, too. I'm just glad we're going together. I'm really glad she was my elbow buddy, since now she's my best friend.

Going back into Mrs. Aldridge class for the last time, I check my cubbyhole that's labeled with my name. Nope, nothing's there. Going into Ms. Hicks's, I place my favorite book, *Flat Stanley*, in a safer place underneath my own desk.

Chapter 5
Connie's Promise

After Missy and I are told that we're going to Ms. Hicks's class, we're also told it's an honor. I don't understand how this is an honor. How's it an honor to go from our class with the big, huge wooden tables and now have to go to a class where everyone sits by themselves? How much fun is that? How will I get any work done when I won't have an elbow buddy? No matter how much I want to squall, it seems that what I say doesn't matter.

Mrs. Aldridge tells us, "Girls, we've discussed this move with your parents already." Did she already talk to my mom? Did she tell her that we have to sit at desks? Doesn't Mom remember that Missy is my best friend? Does this mean that we can't sit at the big tables together, and she won't be my elbow buddy? I don't understand how Mom

could agree to this.

Thinking that the teachers must have read

my mind, Missy is sitting right behind me in Ms.

Hicks's class. Knowing Sarah and Janet from Miss

May's Wednesday ballet class, I don't feel like too

much of a stranger. Missy doesn't know anyone

else, though, besides me. I'll have to make it a

point to include her in everything. I don't want her

to ever feel like me sometimes and be left out.

It's been a week, and the newness and

excitement of first grade is gone. With all the

excitement of moving to a new class, now we have

the same daily routine. We start every day the same

way with our reading circles. In each circle students

take turns reading out loud. This isn't bad since the

circles are small, and the stories go around the circle,

so each child has at least three opportunities to read

every morning. I've decided I like what I call the puzzle books the best. No, there aren't any puzzles in these book, but the story tells a puzzle that the reader has to figure out. It seems I can usually figure out the puzzles of every story by the time it's my second time to read. Ms. Hicks calls these stories mysteries. Some are pretty silly, though. What type of mystery is it if no one can find the cat, but when the book says that the cat is on TV, the cat is only on top of the TV? As the school year moves on, I like it as the stories get more difficult. We are also now reading a paragraph for each read, rather than a sentence. Fridays are the best, when we can read a book we picked out on our own.

Our daily routine continues after reading every morning with math. This is Missy's best part. I can easily add and subtract even if I'm only in the first grade. It's when we get to the double numbers that Missy is ahead of me. It's like she can do these in her head. I don't quite understand when she is solving a double-digit problem, and she says she has to carry. Carry what? How do you carry a number when it's not real? I mean, where does that number go? "Peggy it's OK. We're still ahead doing the single numbers. Just wait until the second grade, and then I'll help you more there."

The school day for first grade is way longer than my preschool days at Saint James. We begin every day with the morning announcements and the pledge of allegiance. After the pledge, that's when school really begins. As I said, we start every day with our reading circles, and then math. Morning recess follows math, and this takes place instead of nap time that we had in preschool. Gosh, my first week is really hard. I miss having my nap, and my mom somehow knew I missed it, too.

Which I didn't know she knew, but somehow, she just knew. Since we get to go outside and play on the front side of the school, I don't even have a chance to fall asleep anymore.

Playing on the front side of the school is called morning recess, which makes sense since it happens in the morning. It's just that morning recess happens in what I call the front of the school, or Rutherford Drive, where Mom drops Katie and me off in the circle by the first-grade hall. On this side, or my side of the school, the monkey bars and obstacle course are found. As first graders, we don't play with those so much, but we hit the sand box. This sits underneath the big shade tree. It's great to go and find what other kids have left hidden or forgotten in the sand. It's also funny to find the squirrels trying to hide things here, too.

Peggy Kohlmeyer

The other side of Barrow Elementary is on the front, but that's for afternoon recess. The older kids get dropped off here on Pinecrest Drive. This is the side that faces the University of Georgia track. Here the school has the swing set and two seesaws. I call this Katie's side of the school since she starts out here in the morning for recess. In the afternoon, we switch, where Katie's class is on my side of the school, but my class is on Katie's side of the school. It's neat to play where the big kids play.

Our day is broken up with lunch. For lunchtime we walk down the hallway and have our restroom break to make sure everyone washes their hands before they eat. After getting into a single-file line in the hallway, we go downstairs to the basement or lunch room. Every day, Mom makes sure I have a PB and J sandwich. Apple jelly is my favorite, but usually it's only grape jam, since it comes in a bigger jar. At the beginning of the school year, almost like it's a secret, Mom tells us if we ever want a school lunch to let her know. Mom tells us there's some type of form that she'll have to fill out for us to go through the lunch line at school. She tells Katie and me in a small voice like there's someone else around to hear. This is weird, since it's only Mom at home with Katie and me. She tells us like it's almost like a secret.

I tell her no. I don't like the surprises that they serve as the school lunch. I especially don't want to guess what the mystery is for the mystery meat for the day. Plus, since I bring my lunch, I get to sit down and finish while some students are still standing in the lunch line. This also means I can get back out on the playground first.

Peggy Kohlmeyer

This is it. It's done. It's the end or closing to my first-grade year. Almost a heavy, somber mood is hovering around Barrow Elementary School. It seems that someone might have died or even passed away, but instead it's the school's own sadness that I feel. Tomorrow, the kids won't be heard shouting in the hallway, and the playgrounds are going to be empty. As it's our last day, we're about to get our end-of-year report cards. Now's the time Ms. Hicks is going to answer my big question. Nope, not whether or not I passed, but where I'm going to be for the following school year.

Standing side by side as always, Missy and I are waiting. With each of us taking a deep breath, we don't question whether or not we've passed, but our teachers for our second-grade year. Now this seems the biggest question ending our first-grade year. Are we going to be together again next year? Will we have the same teacher?

Our hands are shaking with the hesitation as we both hold our report cards. I'm almost scared to open it and find the answer inside. Holding my breath, turning to make sure I have the front cover, almost simultaneously Missy and I both slowly open ours up. I skip over my earned grades for my first year but jump down to the bottom line. Yes, of course, I definitely passed, but even more importantly at this time, glancing to the bottom line for second grade, my teacher next year is…reading it out loud, "I have Miss Tabor."

And Missy almost shrieks into my ear, "I have Miss Tabor's class too! *Yay*!"

Both of us shouting in unison, loud enough for Ms. Hicks to say, "Girls! Use your inside voices," and seeing her grin, knowing she's made

Peggy Kohlmeyer

our summer. First grade for us has meant more than the academics we have learned but meeting new friends.

After the school year closes, summer rolls around, ending where we started before, the week before school starts. Connie is the daughter of one of the officers at the Athens Naval Base. Yes, I said it right. A naval base in Athens, Georgia. Explain that one to me. Knowing that the navy is the military branch that works with the ships and submarines, all located on water. Nope, there is no water on this base except the swimming pool. So how can you explain a ship? Going swimming at this base pool with Daddy's military connection, we can't even have a float. That's not my point, though. Mom's school starts a week before ours, and we can't stay at home by ourselves. Also, with

Connie as our sitter, we feel even safer, since her dad is in the military, too.

Friday is our last day of summer break, and the last day with Connie as our sitter. This week hasn't been bad at all. Playing outside in the morning and reading inside when it gets too hot. Mom signed Katie and me up for the summer reading camp at the Athens Regional Library, and Connie has even driven us to check out some different books. Today, Mom's left some money so Connie can walk with us to Hodgson's Pharmacy. We never get to do this alone, having to cross Lumpkin Street. With Connie as our babysitter, she is also serving as our crossing guard. This is adding to our excitement for our week ending with Connie and our last summer day.

Peggy Kohlmeyer

At Five Points, the five-and-ten convenience store and the Handy Andy gas station are on our side of Lumpkin Street, while Hodgson's Pharmacy is on the opposite side of the street. Remember, the name Five Points is exactly that. Milledge Avenue intersects with Lumpkin Street making four points, while Milledge Circle forms the fifth point for Five Points. These five separate roads merge to make it a five-pointed star. The only reason Mom ever lets us go by ourselves is our promise, with our utmost importance of all promises, to never cross over Lumpkin. This limits us to only going to the Handy Andy. Mom's explanation is that the street is just too busy, the traffic lights always change, or if it's a Georgia football game day, Five Points is constantly a zoo. Today, though, we are totally safe. Connie is with us, and it's the last Friday before we have to start back to school. Even more? Mom gave Connie the money to take us across the street for ice cream at Hodgson's Pharmacy.

With our walking to Five Points, it doesn't mean taking the street like Mom does when she drives, but instead we take our short cuts. Taking Connie on our path, Katie and I first cut through our next-door neighbor Tommy's back yard, and this hits Greenwood Drive. Here we cross over Carlton Terrace, making it to the back-parking lot of the apartments, which is cool, since it's got a carport for us to walk in the shade. This is the spot where our nagging begins. "Connie, come on, you said you would. We've been good all week like you said, and you made that promise on Monday." Katie starts reminding me of the initial behavior expectations for this week and the promise that Connie's made.

On Monday morning, before Mom left for school and with Mom as her witness, Connie tells us, "Girls, I'll read your life lines and tell your fortunes at the end of the week." Almost automatically, I'm holding in my breath. She's going to read my palm? Connie's going to tell me of my future? Then just as quickly, as to knock out all my air, "If there aren't any problems this entire week," she adds. No problems this week? All week? I have to let my breath out slowly, as my disappointment in reality sets in. Mom's evil eye also establishes her own warning about our behavior.

Yes, it's Friday, our last day, and I'm silently thanking Katie for remembering Connie's promise that I've forgotten and even more, for not getting us into trouble.

"Come on, Connie, you promised you would," Katie's reminding her, at the same time reminding me, too.

Quickly, I jump in, agreeing with Katie, "Come on, come on, come on, remember you even promised."

Knowing how important a promise is to us, Connie only stops walking. Turning to Katie, while Katie sticks out the palm of her hand, Connie looks down at it. "Oh, Katie, your life line looks good. It's deep and strong. It's also long. It continues showing you're determined. See this?" Connie's pointing to a specific place on Katie's hand. "This merge has two shorter lines, and it's very thick." Connie adds, "The two shorter lines mean your life might get rocky, but overall due to its thickness, your life will be secure and stable and an overall success." With this said, Katie's grinning from ear to ear. Even though I'm not exactly sure what she said, again I'm a little envious of her. Now it's my turn.

Walking a few steps farther and my mind darting over to the double-dip ice-cream cone at Hodgson's Pharmacy that I'm going to get, Connie asks me for the palm of my hand. "Come on, Peg, it's your turn for a read," not wanting to break her promise to me.

I stick out my hand. Connie looks and looks. "Not good, let me have your other palm." Instead of my right hand, which is the same one Katie had read, I swap out and give her my left hand. Again, looking at my palm, she says, "Nope, let me have your right hand again." Connie's forehead starts bunching up as if she's trying to decipher some secret code. Her own hands become sticky and sweaty. "Peg, I can't read yours. I don't see any of Katie's continuing lines. Your line is cut." Pointing down to my own palm: "Look, they start and stop. So much is going on in your palm. There's nothing consistent…you don't have a solid life line." Still pointing but a little farther along on my palm: "It's showing that something is going to happen, your life line cuts off like an end—."

Catching her breath, she says "But wait, it does pick up on the other side." I look up at her with curiosity and question, so she guards herself. "I don't want to make a prediction that's going to be wrong," Connie says, as she folds over my fingers into my palm like she is trying to cover up what she's just read. Now quickly dropping my hand, as Katie bursts out asking me, "Are you going to get the same rocky road ice cream again?" to erase any negative thoughts I might have in my mind.

Peggy Kohlmeyer

Chapter 6
Ending Second Grade

My second-grade year at Barrow Elementary School is pretty much the same. I'm used to sitting at a desk, and I'm used to Ms. Tabor's daily routine. Math does come first this year though, after our pledge of allegiance, followed by reading. This year, we don't have circles that we read in; instead, we read on our own and earn points. Sarah is in my second-grade class this year, too. She's my main competitor for which one of us is leading in our class.

As second graders, we do have more freedom. Ms. Tabor doesn't line us up to go to the restrooms; we have to sign our names and take her wooden pass with her name on it and go by ourselves. We're told that this is a freedom, even if it comes with the responsibility of trust. She says her pass shows everyone else where we belong.

Going to the restroom by myself is fun or my daily adventure. Watching the other kids, I don't take as long as they do, so this allows me the extra time to go down the second- and third- grade wing to the center rotunda, making it back to the first-grade hall. The first time I did this, I did get scared. I mean, I'm still going to the restroom, but just not the one closest to our room. I also have to pass under His picture. His picture is the big picture that hangs underneath the glass ceiling in the rotunda. Katie told me that it's David C. Barrow, and he's watching us. His is the only picture there, and it's always staring at you no matter which way you're walking. He's looking at everything you do.

I can see why. He's David C. Barrow, the owner of this building, and he might just be watching us to make sure we take care of the school for him. It's pretty neat, since they named it after him, Barrow Elementary. The first time I passed under His picture, I told my mom when I got home. I guess it's OK since she laughed when I told her about him looking at me. "The owner of the school, Peg? Who's that?" she asked me, and I told her about his picture. "No, Peggy, he's not the owner, but the school was named after him. The school building is owned by Clarke County, the county where we live. He's one of the former presidents at the University of Georgia. He's also the university president who allowed woman to first attend. Your school is named after him since he had such a positive influence on the University of Georgia." I take this as Mom's OK, and now I make it my requirement to pass by and say hi to him every day with Ms. Tabor's restroom pass. If Mom's university had the owner of my school working there for her, I owe him my respect, at the school named after him.

Almost as a repeat of the end of school from last year, once again Missy and I are standing side by side as Miss Tabor passes out our final report cards for the second-grade. I'm crossing my fingers, wanting to repeat the same magic that happened this time last year for us. Can Missy and I pass the double luck from sharing our second-grade year to triple luck and have the same third-grade teacher next year?

Opening my report card, it says that I've been placed in Miss Greer's third-grade class. Looking at Missy, she's only crying. What? *There's no way she failed!* Opening her report card, of course she's passed, and I let out a huge sigh of relief, but looking at it, there's not a teacher's name for her third-grade year. Joining in with Missy and us both crying with my voice stammering, I finally ask Miss Tabor, "What's wrong? She passed, she's got marks on all the "excellent," but she doesn't have a teacher for next year."

"Oh," is the only answer that I hear Miss Tabor say, already knowing Missy is moving.

Summer is long, and it's very hot, but Hope Avenue is still the perfect street to raise the perfect family. With Mom, we're getting closer as perfect, especially since our house sits at the halfway point of our neighborhood block. Sitting on our front porch facing the street, directly to your right, it's Tommy and his parents who are our next-door neighbors. There is a row of bushes that separates our garages, but we can still cut through to their back yard. Next to Tommy's house, two houses up is Mrs. Stephenson's house, with her two sons, Johnny and

Teddy. She's Mom's closet friend. She has so many trees in her front and backyard, there is no place to play. The last house on the end, next to Mrs. Stephenson, is Linda and her parents. Her yard is uneven, so all we can do is sit on her front porch steps, which isn't bad when it's been a long day, and count the cars driving by. Linda has an older sister. She's so much older that I think she's already married.

Going to my front porch again sitting and facing the street, on the opposite left-hand side at the very end of the street is Tia and her little brother Jay. Their last name is Flanagan, and she has a mom and a dad. They have a huge back yard without a fence, but the pecans that fall hurt anyone's bare feet to walk on them. Across from the Flanagan's, also at that end, Stacey lives. Stacey has two parents, but they seem older. I mean, gray-haired older. We rarely see them outside except for when her dad mows the yard. Stacey even has her own tree house, but it's only fun to climb up and down. Once you get to it, there's nothing to do. Yes, other people fill in the other houses, but these people we label mystery people. When we point to their houses, we call them "those people," since we don't ever see them, or they don't have kids, so we don't know who they are.

Having our house in the center of the block, it's the place for the kids on our street to all meet. Our front yard? It's big, it's wide, and it's open. Yes, in our front yard, daily decisions are made.

Tommy's the oldest and therefore basically the leader, but sometimes he even takes the role of dictator. With the Memorial Park pool only, a mile or so away, he opens up with, "Who wants to go to the pool today?"

"I do."

"Yeah, me, too."

"I'll go."

"Count me in."

This quickly starts our plan, but he also asks the inevitable deciding question we always have to answer, "Who's going to take us?" which definitely squashes his idea. Knowing that each mom is going to tell us, "Get there on your own," while we all remember it's a longer trip walking back, since you are pool tired and dripping wet.

This leaves us with the only other option of whose turn it is to decide what we're going to do for the rest of the day. What's our next step? Almost automatically. the list starts by location on our street. Since Linda lives at the end, she goes first. She has badminton rackets, but we've already lost the birdie. We think it's in a tall tree or up on her roof. Tia is on the opposite end of the street,

and she has horseshoes, but they'll ruin the grass

and tear up everyone's front yard. Then Ted's

house is next to Linda's, and he has a soccer ball.

The last time we played a game, it was in the

center of the street, which ended with sudden death

for "a stupid idea," labeled by Stacey's father.

Today, we're down to two choices: a game of tag

or Tommy, who is the only one with a football and

our next-door neighbor.

Diverging our plan of action and calling on

Tommy to go back to his house to get his ball,

we've all agreed to meet back at my house at 9:00

a.m. Gathering water bottles and sports drinks and

tapping the garden hose for the necessary pregame

preparations, our morning is finally taking place.

After reporting to Mom up at Mrs. Stephenson's

house with our decision to stay in the neighborhood,

I'm meeting back in our front yard. Suddenly I hear a swoosh, while feeling a whack upside my head. It knocks me down but not hard enough to knock me out. Gritting my teeth with the pain, it's only "Ughhh" that I express. With Katie nowhere around for me to blame, Tommy yells out to me, "You shouldn't walk in the line of the ball," as if it's my fault. Seeing Tommy's football rolling down our driveway, I realize why he's blaming me. His warm-up toss hit me upside my head. Shrugging it off, Tommy's acting like the stud he thinks he is since he's the senior quarterback of the Clarke Central High School state champs.

Mom, getting the report and running out of Mrs. Stephenson's house, yells out, "Peg, are you all right?"

Tommy's mom gently tells me to "Hold still, let me look," while she's placing an ice bag to the right of my eye. Wondering how bad I'm going to look, Mom only says, "Wow, that's really, really going to bruise," confirming my concern.

The next day, our neighborhood morning meeting is politely interrupted with Mom grinning largely, planting two huge dogwood trees right in the front of our house. She tells our crew that one is for Katie while the other one is for me. Her silent vengeance blocks all the future games that we'll never play, ending whatever popularity our empty and open front yard ever had, and I'm still waiting on that apology from Tommy.

Looking now at our backyard, it's almost divided in half. The lower half of the back yard is grassy and easy on my bare feet. Starting on the left-hand side from our back door, our garage is detached and separated almost twenty-five feet away, where it elevates in a land rise up from the house. From the garage the driveway is paved all the way down to the street. Rows of Mom's irises border the edge of the backyard, covering the bent-over old wire fence. Next to this border of Mom's irises comes the backyard grass, where our yard actually begins.

This lower grassy part isn't deep or wide enough for anything to happen. This grassy area is also narrow and too close to our house, so a bad pitch of a ball would shatter or break a window. On the other hand, the upper half is only dirt since a huge, old oak tree broadly branches out, blocking all the sun. This old oak tree is so big that trying to reach around it and hug it, I can't reach Katie's fingers or hands. Also, this tree is so tall, I can't even reach the lowest limb to climb up in it. But this is our new place to play, and I only have to mention, "Who's going to get sick first?" as the invitation to play in our backyard, since Katie and I are the only kids in our neighborhood with a tire swing.

For this game, the point is to make the other person sick. To start this game, everyone playing is touching their fingertips on our backdoor screen. On the shout of "Go!" it's the quickest dash and first to reach and slap the tire swing rope. Going up the elevation or rise in the yard, those with weak lungs are winded and eliminated. You always want to be first, since this is the winner who now has control of the game and gets to make all the calls of who spins the first rider in the swing. If you can't walk after the spin, the spinner automatically wins.

Each time it's Katie's win, a loud, almost automatic sigh escapes from our friends. She's the toughest person to turn the tire swing, making it tight enough to guarantee the rider's going to get sick. And each time, she always picks me.

Hearing our friends sigh, I feel their relief, knowing they won't get sick this round. Hemming and hawing and "Why me?" is all I say, eventually giving in.

"It's the rules of the game" is what I hear. Knowing this, I give in, already regretting how sick I'm going to be after this round. As you can tell, our backyard is perfect.

Mom's friend Mrs. Stephenson has a friend, and her friend has four kids, with one daughter, Heather. Even though Heather doesn't live on our street, Hope Avenue, she's only a walking distance away and another half block down Milledge Terrace to her backyard driveway. Her front yard faces Milledge Heights, with a creek running through it. With all these connections Heather almost automatically becomes our friend. With Mom

Peggy Kohlmeyer

planting the dogwood trees in the front yard,

Heather's friendship opens our playing terrain. This

summer days are a tradeoff. Either we're at Heather's

house at her creek, out in the front of her yard, or at

our house in our backyard, on the tire swing. Needless

to say, if we are not at one place, we're at the other, or

walking barefoot on the hot pavement of the street in

between. Also, Heather completes our lineup for

elementary grade levels. Tia is going into the second

grade, while I'm going into the third grade. Heather is

going into the fourth grade, while Katie is going into

the fifth grade. As you see, we're set looking out for

the others, having almost all the elementary grades

covered and also establishing our summer pecking

order.

When Mom announces that she's running up

to Bell's grocery store, it's not that she's going on an

actual run. It's her code word that means Katie and I

can't leave our yard until she comes home. We don't mind, especially this time. We've just gotten a stupendous big slide. It's from my old preschool at Saint James, and they needed to get rid of it. It's so big that it even took three men in a truck to haul it up to our backyard. Some members of the church brought it over this morning, so when Mom says she's going to Bell's, we're set. I mean, it's the big, stand-alone kind of slide that's not even attached to a swing set. Again and again, we slide, climb back up the ladder, and slide again. Katie and I love it. This time with Mom at Bell's, we don't even bat an eye that she's gone.

After going down the slide about twenty more times, Katie acts like she's playing super smart and gets a sheet of wax paper from our kitchen cabinet. Sitting on it, she slides down going super-fast. I'm looking at her aghast at what she's dared to do, "Oh, that's only you!" Thinking to myself she's going to get herself killed.

"Oh, you're scared!"

"No, I'm not. I only don't want to copy you." Sticking my tongue out to make sure this registers to her.

By this time Heather's walking up the driveway. As number two in our pecking order, Heather won't let Katie outdo her. Without hesitation Heather grabs some wax paper, too. She slides down the slide, making sure Katie knows that she's successful with what she's been challenged to do. The two repeatedly go down the slide again and again. I'm getting bored sitting on the back porch concrete step watching them. I don't want to give in and go inside, but it's baking hot now. The sun's straight up, meaning it's only going to get hotter and the metal of the slide is almost too hot to touch.

"Come on, let's move it over to the shade," Katie suggests, "and once we get it off the grass, it's going to get easier to move across the dirt," as she begins to pull on it. With Katie on one side and Heather on the other, standing in front, I navigate them to under the largest limb of our backyard oak tree.

Now, with the slide in the shade, it's not a slide anymore; now it serves as a ladder. It's a new game we can play. Katie's new challenge is climbing up the slide stairs like a ladder, standing at the top, and reaching across to touch the limb of our tallest tree. Following the same pecking order since Katie did it, Heather's attempt is next, and after Heather, me. Following our designated order of one, two, and three. With Katie up first, she displays no fear. Simple enough, she climbs the ladder and *SMACK* marking the designated spot on

the tree limb.

"OK now, Heather, your turn to go."

Heather is looking up with a little fear in her face;

my own fear begins to grow watching her hesitation

as she rests her foot on the bottom step. Katie

reassures her, "What? You've climbed this ladder

before," as her final words of encouragement.

Hearing Heather draw in a deep breath,

"Ooooooh," climbing to the top, I then hear

SMACK, as evidence of her success on reaching the

lowest limb. Next, it's left to number three, or me.

Looking straight up the backside of our new slide, I see

the summer blue sky beyond the limbs of our tree, beyond the slide's top step. With a visual reminder of exactly how high our new slide goes, that's the worst thing I could have done. Refocusing and stabilizing myself, now grabbing the ladder.

"Come on Peggy, it's your turn next. You chickened out earlier, don't be a wimp again" are the words of encouragement I hear from my older sister.

Trying to ignore her, Heather gives me comfort. "Peggy, remember you've climbed it out there," pointing to its former location. "It's still the same, only now you have to raise your hand to reach the tree."

OK. That's all it is this time. Just raising my hand to touch the tree, I'm telling myself and feeling a little better.

Peggy Kohlmeyer

Thinking of a strategy. Is it one step at a time, taking a deep breath in between, or me rushing to the top, successfully popping the upside of that tree? *Thud, thud, thud, thud* is all I hear, from the clunking noise that I'm making going up. Reaching to the top with a subtle *pop*. "Whew! I'm done with that," I tell myself, breathing now, not capable of making any other thoughts as I have to get back down.

Do I get any congratulations, fanfare, or celebration for my achievement? Nope, not from cohort's number one or number two, only a new game or an even more difficult strategy develops as my reward. Heather and Katie are now inching the slide over some more. This time, the new challenge is to touch the edge of our garage roof.

Following the same pecking order: one, Katie; two, Heather; and three, me. Thinking to myself, "Oh, this one's going to be easy," as I evaluate the height difference between the two and noticing to my relief that the garage is actually lower than the tree limb. Just as this is said, Katie's already returning to the bottom of the slide. Without a doubt, this is followed by Heather and then me.

Picking up on my personal success and to continually challenge me, Katie has to go back up. This time, to make it that much more difficult, Katie climbs the slide stairs, and instead of touching the garage roof, she uses the tree limb to raise herself up to the top.

What? Doing a double take. Katie's now on the roof of our car garage! While she's grasping each roof shingle tightly, crawling to the roof's ridge, peeking over, waving her hand, I only hear her say hey to Tommy's mom, as if she's right outside in her backyard.

Heather, as number two and not wanting to be left out, does exactly the same. The two of them, now gloating together, point out to each other what they see. "Look over to the Flanagan's yard," way down at the end of our street.

"Yeah, I see it. See where Jay left his bike on top of the trampoline?"

"Look up on Linda's roof."

"So that's all the badminton birdies!"

"But do you see what else?

"Oh gosh, look what's next to it!"

"Where it belongs…out of reach!"

"Hey, Peg! You've got to come up here." Only leaving me more curious.

"It's Tommy's football over on Linda's house!"

Returning from her grocery run, Mom pulls up beside the house. Quickly, Katie's crouching down, while Heather's also trying to flatten herself out. Neither one of them can afford the trouble they'll each get into if they get caught. I hear Mom getting out of the car, yelling, "Y'all be careful out there" to let us know she's home. With a Bell's grocery store bag in either arm, focusing instead of her own steps, Mom can't glance up. That's OK, since now that she's back, there's no reason for me to be afraid.

Seeing Mom back home is my encouragement, so I hurry up the last two top steps on the ladder of our new slide. I'm finally having a feeling of personal success, breaking into a cold sweat. Using the tree limb to pull myself up, my hands are shaking. I ignore my fear as a chill goes down my spine, even though it's another hot July.

Peggy Kohlmeyer

I'm only following what Katie and Heather have already done, trying so hard to be like them.

It's great. I'm finally at the top of our garage roof to sit with Katie and Heather. Quickly, my feeling of euphoria ends, as a new problem creeps in; I'm totally too scared to move! I don't want to go up to the Pike and look over and see Tommy's backyard. I already know what's there. Hitting our asphalt driveway could only hurt as my body smacked it. I don't want to climb up to the front of the garage either. I mean, what if I look over and fall?

Waiting for what seems like forever, Katie and Heather finally inch back down from the Pike where they were. But it's like I'm not even here. They're not even speaking to me. Instead, Katie's doing everything in reverse. First she holds on to the tree branch and swings back over to touch the slide.

I'm looking at her; she's getting down so easily. Heather, or number two in line, is next, and she does the same thing. First the tree branch, followed by successfully swinging her body to the slide.

Me? I only sit.

I still can't move.

Sitting and sitting for what seems forever. Katie and Heather are on the ground and now. Katie's laughing. Standing by the garage and next to the slide she's telling Heather something. I can't hear them, but now Heather's also laughing.

Wait! What are they doing?

They're pulling on the slide. Katie's on the right, and Heather's on the left. They're moving it away. Heather's helping Katie tug at the slide, moving it far enough away. They both look up at me innocently. Now they're enjoying a different success

Peggy Kohlmeyer

since the slide is originally where it was placed in
our backyard.

Panic hits me. How am I going to get
down? How am I ever going to get off our garage
roof?

"Katie, what am I going to do? Heather!
Wait! I can't get down!"

"Oh yes, you can. Just jump!"

"Jump?" I'm asking myself.

"Yeah, jump" is Katie's only answer,
challenging me as if she's reading my mind.

"Jump from up here?" I now say out loud.

Jump from our garage roof? Did Katie just
actually shout for me to jump from our garage?
What's she thinking now? She's crazier than me!
Prancing down our grassy slope to our back porch,
Katie's touching the screen door. "*Wait*! *Stop*!" I

call out, panicking and shouting, "Come back, just tell me how to jump!"

Running back, Katie simply shouts, "Think of yourself as Wonder Woman. Like the woman on TV."

Now I realize there's really no hope for me. Katie and Heather begin to giggle together more loudly.

Wonder Woman? She wants me to think that I'm Wonder Woman? What superhuman powers do I have? Even more, who does she think she is? Telling me to think I'm some Wonder Woman from a TV show? "Never fear," I try to reassure myself. Sitting up here, I'm now at a personal loss of my own self esteem.

I look around and confirm that the slide is too far away. My other option, the tree branch that I used to pull myself up, will only drop me farther out away from the roof. Looking and searching, I see there aren't any other options. No matter what, I'll still hit the ground. Not pausing to take even a breath, all I can do is jump. *Thud*!

"What? What are you doing?" Mom's screaming out her lungs, running out the back door, hearing me land with such a thud. When she gets to my side, there's suddenly a deafening silence all around. I can't move. I can only cry.

"She…told…me…to…jump," I hear myself stammering. My crying and breathing are both hurting, getting heavier and harder.

Katie's expressionless look is in her defense, adding, "I didn't think she was going to do it. I was just going to go inside." Almost acknowledging her guilt but quickly adding in her own protection, "I promise, I swear, I was only going inside for a minute," as her lower lip start to tremble. Glancing around, Mom sees that Heather is gone and can't come to Katie's defense.

Mom is holding me tightly, helping me up to stand while Katie's quietly inching away. "Don't you even think about moving," Mom threatens, pointing a finger at her.

Only as we pass each other so quietly for Mom not to hear, Katie curtly whisper, "You just didn't believe. You didn't believe you were Wonder Woman. So this is all your fault," with Mom slowly walking with me to the back door.

You bet after this event I'm totally done with number one and number two, or the both of them, for this summer. I don't even make our neighborhood morning meetings anymore. I'm not missing anything after realizing it's always me getting the raw end of their deal. Now my only option is to hang out around our house. Actually, this isn't so bad, since Mom is home for our summer, too.

Our house is the perfect size, not too big and not too small. I do have my own bedroom, which is painted green, which I'm told is to increase some type of inner creativity. My room is on the front side of the house facing the street, which only gets the morning sun. Katie's bedroom is on the back side of the house and is painted blue. The name of her paint color is "Cool Blue." For me this is only a mind game since every afternoon, her room is no way cool and hotter than the outside of the house.

This heat explains why it's hard for us to stay home. We could simply turn on our AC, but it's only a window unit for the living room. Asking Mom why she doesn't turn it on, she goes into an explanation with money. Here she compares the cost for a gallon of ice cream to the cost of the AC for an hour. For this reason, I don't mind the summertime heat. Ice cream wins, and anyway, the heat gives us the best reason to get out of our house and go somewhere else.

Dealing with the afternoon heat, Mom drives us all to the Athens Regional Library every Wednesday. At the library, this is our opportunity to check out or renew our library books. The library has a summer reading camp. This is the kind of camp that I really enjoy, a summer camp just for me. At this camp, I don't have to move; I just sit and read, and even better, this puts a break in our week, and we get to read in their air conditioning, too!

At this camp the best camper reads the most books. I feel I'm doing great, since the list of the books that I've read is more than filled. Bored with the third-grader books, I've moved up my reading to Katie's fifth-grader list. These are definitely more fun to read and make me feel like I'm a super-secret spy. By reading her books, I'm catching a glimpse of what I have to understand when I'm Katie's age. My biggest difficulty though? Waiting for Katie to finish with the books that she has and checking them out myself.

Right now, *Tom Sawyer* makes the top of my favorite book list. I had to sneak it out from Katie's stack of books to return to the library at our front door. This book is old. Not only old in print, but it's an older book to read, meaning it's for an older audience without having pictures in it. This book's cover is also dull brown in its binder. These types of books are sometimes the best, since so many other people have already read them, and they're still around. Mom tells me, "Peg they're just so popular to read, they have to get a new cover." Opening the book, it lets out a creaking noise. This tells me, "Oh, Katie didn't read this, she didn't even open it up." Now this marks Tom Sawyer as a book that Katie hasn't read, which makes it that much better. I can add it to my reading list instead of her.

Starting the first chapter, Tom Sawyer is the kid I want to be. He's curious and sneaky and gets out of trouble just as he's getting into it again. Although Tom does have me perplexed enough, having to ask, "Mom, will you beat me with a switch?" Not thinking she heard me, asking her again, "Mom, will you beat me with a switch?"

Putting her book down, she gawks at me. "Peg, what are you talking about a switch?"

"I'm reading *Tom Sawyer*, and he gets a spanking with a switch. You only hit us with your hand. I want to know what really being in trouble is like, and I want you to spank me with a switch."

Hearing Mom laugh, I take it this as her answer. That's OK, I'm ready for the third grade.

Chapter 7
Third Grade!

My mom is a teacher in a library, her school's library. She works every day with the kids at her school and checks out their school library books. Since she's a teacher and her calendar is like ours, we share the same weekends and holidays off. The big difference is she starts back a week before Katie and I have to go back to school. This is called her preplanning. Mom doesn't work in Athens; she has to drive every day or commute to Commerce, Georgia. To save money she meets fellow teachers to carpool. This means that she has to get up earlier than us every school day and come home later than us every school day, too.

Katie and I know that when Mom starts back to school, we start back soon or a week later. It also means that once again for a week, we're supposed to have that all-day babysitter. Going into the third grade after jumping from our garage roof, I don't feel like Wonder Woman at all. I also think I'm too old and responsible for someone to watch me for the day. I've learned from my mistake.

Mom opens this issue again about a babysitter when she asks us, "Who's it going to be this year?"

Katie pipes in, not mentioning Connie from last year. "Mom, if we take care of ourselves, think of the money you'll save."

Mom quickly and vehemently disagrees, saying that our safety is more important than money. But knowing that we've moved beyond the babysitter, she's more accepting of my suggestion of spending the week at the local YMCA day camp. The reality of it all is that when the school year really starts, we'll only have Mom to ourselves on Saturday and Sunday.

No doubt the first day of my third-grade class at Barrow School is empty without Missy. Math is harder, and I'll really miss Missy since she isn't here to help me with the double-digit math. Janet from my Wednesday ballet class is sitting in front of me, which is nice since she is someone I know. Ballet class is now on Monday and Wednesday, and the four of us—Barbara, Mary, Janet, and I—make the walk together. Sara moved over the summer, but I'm not sure where. Ballet is still fun. This year, we'll have a ballet show at Christmastime. Pretty neat, too; all the people of Athens are invited.

Wednesdays I've marked as great like my double-dip days. It's double the treat like the double-dip ice cream cone Mom gets us when we visit Hodgson's Pharmacy. Why two dips? So the flavors will last forever and remembering them the next time we go back again. And with ice cream

for me it's always got to be two: rocky road and

pistachio almond fudge. But for me at school, if it's

Wednesday, it's a day marked for ballet, which I'll

call my first dip, rocky road. My second dip is for

me meeting with Miss Gardner, and she's the

pistachio.

I'm first introduced to Miss Gardner as she

meets me at Miss Greer's classroom door as we're

returning from morning recess. "Peggy, you're

going to go with Mrs. Gardner, and she is going to

work with you on your speech."

Speech? Am I supposed to give a speech?

This is something that Mom watches on TV from

the president or even the people who report the

evening news. I'm only in third grade, how am I

going to give a speech? Yes, this I'm calling my

second dip for my double-dip day, since two things

are going to be happening for me like my ice cream cone.

Walking with Miss Gardner down the empty school hallways, we reach the library. Sitting down at one of the wooden library tables in the far back corner, near the wall, Miss Gardner tells me that my *R*s are not formed correctly when they come out of my mouth. My *R*s aren't formed right? I didn't know there was even a wrong way of making an *R*. Now I'm really puzzled, so what's to make it right?

If I'm thirsty and need some water, I ask for it, but it comes out *wa-urrs*. Growing up, Poder is always Poder, but I didn't know that he's actually supposed to be grand*father*. I know what people are saying, and people who know me know what I am saying, but now I'm meeting Miss Gardner, or *Mrs.* Gardner if I'm correctly sounding it out.

Holding cards with pictures, Miss Gardner waits for me to copy and repeat what she says, pointing to each picture. The first one up is easy, "*Cat*," and I reply, "*Cat*." Then "*Mop*," and I reply "*Mop*." Followed by "*Moon*."

Afterward, while smiling, nodding her head toward me, she says, "Good job." OK I've got this, but now my fear sets in as Miss Garner's holding her next set of cards: *Run, Work, Ramp*.

She says I'm supposed to do what we did before, and I'm to repeat each word after her. Starting the first one with a soft, fluid voice, I hear her as she says "*Run*."

Now listening I say "*Wun*." I'm not right, but she goes to the next: "*Work*."

Again, knowing the word that I've heard and knowing what I'm supposed to say, "*Wok*" is all I hear myself say.

Without hesitation Miss Gardner moves to the last card, pointing to the picture. *"Ramp."* Smiling at me with encouragement, her head slightly tilts. Carefully listening to what word comes out.

"Wamp," I only pronounce as I see her faintly frown.

Looking me in the eye, Miss Gardner politely says, "Now let's start."

Let's start? Isn't that what I've been doing? Placing her cards face down, and wanting me to shift my focus, she's now pointing to her tongue. Her tongue is pressing on the roof of her mouth. She's demonstrating to me how she forms the sounds and how they come out sounding right. Giving me a mirror so I can see what's going on in my mouth. I'm holding it so I can copy her. I don't like what I see. When I try and form the *R*s as Miss Gardner does, my tongue isn't forming the same shape as hers. My mind

tells me to copy, but my tongue isn't doing it.

Looking up at her, she's demonstrating the right way

and the sound that follows her is "*Rrrr.*" I'm

practicing each word, saying, "*Rrrun, Worrrk,*

Rrramp," each time looking in the mirror.

I hear myself as I quietly say, "*Wun.*"

Trying again, "*Wun.*" Focusing not only my

tongue, but also my lips. Each time looking at Miss

Gardner as she sounds it out and then in the mirror

to copy what she's done, trying to sound it out.

Again, and again, and finally, "*Run.*"

Oh, I get it now; *Mrs.* Gardner is helping

me work on my *speech.*

It was 1929 when David C. Barrow died,

and our elementary school was named in his

honor. At some time, it was an actual fort before it

was a school. With that you know I'm serious

when I'm saying our school has been around for years. That being said, this building is old, and I'm meaning really old, so we don't have central air. Since we're in May, the Athens summer heat is set to bake, so just imagine how hot our classes get in the afternoon.

I'm still in Miss Greer's class, but now it's *Mrs.* Greer's class; I'm embarrassed thinking of what I'd been saying all year. Still having recess this year, I know that in the morning, it's on the south side of the school, or rather what I used to call the first graders' side. Our second or afternoon recess time is on the north side of the school, or the older kids side with the swing set. Regardless of which side of the school, it's a lot harder for us having fun when the sun's straight up.

This afternoon, Mrs. Greer is outside the classroom with us. Even worse, to save on energy the teachers have been told to turn their classroom fans off unless we're in the room. If she's outside, it's hot, and if she's inside without any AC, it's just about as hot or even hotter. It's almost a no-win situation for her. Standing in the shade of the trees, she's fanning herself with whatever papers she's finished grading.

After standing in what little shade's around, everyone finally seems to adjust to the outside heat and starts playing when Jack yells, "Tag."

Tag's a game for anyone and everyone with never being "it." When you're it, the goal is running to catch someone else and tag them. Hiding behind the tree that really isn't big enough to cover me, I'm feeling this heat. Jack sees me and tags me. Now I'm it. When Jack was it, I could see all the other kids and where they were hiding. Now since I'm it and it's my turn, I just can't find anyone. Finally,

I'm giving up and end up standing next to Mrs. Greer.

"Peg, you're looking so hot" are the only words I hear her say. Smiling in acknowledgment, I simply nod my head to agree. Mrs. Greer blows her whistle as her signal to the class that it's time for us to go back inside the school building. Seeing everyone slip out of where they were hiding, I'm telling myself to remember these sneaky places where I need to try to hide next time.

Now I'm feeling the heat hit me more while I'm trying to stand still for everyone else in our class to line up. Waiting on the others, I glance back, looking over my shoulder at the playground. All those special places to hide don't seem as important in my memory right now. I can't even remember what I told myself to remember and why I'm bothering to turn around to look.

Peggy Kohlmeyer

Putting my head down on my desk back in class I hear Mrs. Greer ask, "Janet, will you go and get Peggy a sweater? She's got a chill." The thought of borrowing someone else's clothes makes me ill, but fighting my teeth not to chatter, I ignore it. With only a slight hesitation—anyone's clothing is going to feel better, I'm so cold

Hearing the afternoon announcements on the school PA system, I'm remembering it's Wednesday, or my double-dip day. Oh, double-dip day. I've marked it as pistachio almond fudge for Mrs. Gardner, but what's the other dip for? Pistachio almond or is it Miss Gardner? Did I see her? What speech did she make me practice? Double dip? What's the other flavor? I'm confused while angry since I can't focus to remember this for myself.

"Peggy, who can we call to come pick you up?" I'm hearing the question, but that's not Miss Gardner's voice that I was just thinking about. "Peggy, Peggy, you've got a fever. Who can we call to come pick you up at school?" Making the connection and realizing Mrs. Greer's voice is by my desk leaves me to wonder where did Miss Gardner go? Didn't I see her today? Pick me up? Pick me up? Who wants to pick me up?

"Peggy, listen, who do I call to come get you at the school?"

Trying to answer her, my teeth are chattering as the chill on my body gets stronger. "My mom's at her school in Commerce. If something is wrong, you need to call my Mimi."

"Janet, if you'll go to the front office and let them know…

Peggy Kohlmeyer

Peggy, Peggy. As you said, we tried to call your grandmother. We tried your Mimi, but she didn't answer the phone."

As I pause the thought hits me. Oh, it's Wednesday, it's my double dip day. Now thinking out loud. "It's Wednesday."

"Yes, dear, it's Wednesday."

They're giving me a long pause, waiting for me to finish. Remembering that on the day that I have dance, Katie has horseback riding out in Watkinsville. It's Mimi who picks Katie up after school and takes her riding, while Mom picks me up after ballet.

Hearing her voice again. "Peggy, who can we call to pick you up? You're going to need to go to the hospital. You've got to see a doctor."

A doctor? Mrs. Greer's strong words put me into a state of shock. Pick me up? Pick me up?

Someone needs to pick me up? Someone needs to pick me up and take me to the doctor? Not Mom? Not Mimi…panicking now, I can't even think, and I don't know how to answer.

"Peg, who is it that we can call?"

Think! Think! Trying to think of the phone numbers of who else to call. Thinking, mentally I'm going down the list of numbers posted by the phone in our kitchen. Ours is at the top, while Mimi's is next. After Mimi's is Mrs. Stephenson's, but that's pointless with her at work. Heather's phone number is there, but that's one of Katie's numbers for her friend, and I don't even know it.

Mentally I'm going down the list trying to remember…and then, Tia! Oh yeah, Tia's number is the one at the bottom of our list since it's new. Remembering and sharing it fast enough, fearing that I am going to forget. "Mrs. Gear, Mrs. Gear, three-five-three, two-five-two-seven," I'm hearing

myself say. "It's Tia's number. Tia, my friend who

goes to Saint Joseph's school. Her number is three-

five-three, two-five-two-seven." Pausing after each

number, not to pierce my tongue with the

chattering of my teeth.

It's as if I've broken some important secret

code by knowing the password. Having the feeling

of success of finally remembering a number, I put

my head back down on my desk. Now all of a

sudden, delirium and distress are creeping in, and

my mind is scaring me. What if no one can pick me

up? Tia Flanagan can't drive. Who is at her house

that can come to the school? What if I'm left here?

What if I have to spend the night? With the lights

out? With no one else here, will the ghosts try and

find me? Ghosts? Are there really any ghosts that

live here? This building is so old. What if I see

them? Do I hide in the cloak closet, so no one will see me? What happens if no one can come and pick me up? How will I get home? Where will I sleep? How will I take a bath? What happens if I can't make it to the girls' restroom? Will I have to stay in Mrs. Greer's room? My own delusions are dashing around in my mind worrying me now.

Wrapped in a blanket in the front seat of Mr. Flanagan's car. "Sir, we really appreciate you transporting Peggy to the emergency room." Hearing our principal. "Her mom is going to meet you there." The principal looking between Mr. Flanagan and me. "Little lady, you're one fortunate young girl to have someone in your neighborhood like this."

Clenching my jaw tightly so my teeth won't chatter, I barely mumble "Thank you," requiring all my effort and breath.

Peggy Kohlmeyer

In the emergency room at Saint Mary's hospital, with the ice in plastic bags wrapping my body frame, I'm freezing as they try to cool my internal body heat. My teeth are chattering against a plastic wedge in my mouth, helping me not to bite my tongue. From the corner of my eye I see Mom talking to Mr. Flanagan. Fading in and out, I keep missing parts of what's being said. I'm trying so hard to get her to say, "Thank you," but I can't get my mouth to move. Still thinking so hard for Mom to say, "Thank you," not for her but for me. Silently I say, "Mr. Flanagan, I'm so glad it was your number for me to remember if this follows the lines in my hand."

Chapter 8
Katie's Knife

Hope Avenue has pretty much lived up to its name for me. I think living here has given Mom the stability that she needs. With Mom's stability, she's gained more independence, and this is seen with her daily commute to her school. For me I don't understand that this is her chosen career. I only know that she is gone every school day and doesn't carry the label as a stay-at-home mom. For me this is a two-fold gain: Mom's having a career and making money, while Katie and I get the sense of a strong work ethic. Having Katie and me to provide for, she really didn't have much of a choice. Almost following the tree of life, since she's working full time, there's also a greater sense of her financial independence. With her as the trunk of the tree and Katie and me as her branches, her salary can allow our lifestyle to flourish. I feel that this street and neighborhood have given my mom hope, which trickles down to me.

With a teacher's pay occurring once a month, instead of biweekly, and child support from Daddy, we're fortunate that Mom's established a livable routine. Mom calls this her budget. This takes place on the first of each and every month. When Mom's in her bedroom and the ledger is out on her bed, this is the signal of utmost importance not to disturb her. Since she's gotten her paycheck, we've got to be quiet, as Mom's paying the bills.

As soon as Mom gets paid and with no significant food left in our house, a grocery store trip is always a must. It's this first-of-the-month spree that Katie and I both can have our "wants," rather than only shopping for the "needs." Here,

Mom's monthly budget basically agrees with the extra purchases.

For Katie, it's always a large bag of Ruffles potato chips and a liter of Coke. For her, both of these are gone in a day. For me it's the old-fashioned original Oreo cookies and a gallon of chocolate ice cream. Not the plain chocolate, but chocolate ice cream trying to match my favorite flavor from Hodgson's Pharmacy with the taste of rocky road with almonds and marshmallows. Of course, I ration these two favorites, which last me a week to ten days. But what's for dinner on the evening of a grocery store trip? It's the fried chicken that Mom's cooking to mark the celebration of getting paid and the beginning of the month. Mom is frying the chicken and all its parts in the afternoon, so she'll also have enough time to prepare her own splurge of liver and onions. Thankfully, she only stinks up our house with this disgusting smell once a month.

By the end of the month, when there are five weekends instead of four, Mom's budget is usually tapped. Maybe it's not what we want to eat, or even more don't want to make the effort to eat, but what we have to eat with the limited selection of food choices marking the end of the month. This is first evident in our school lunches. Instead of me packing my faithful PB and J sandwich, I call upon my own creativity to get by. This is usually fulfilled with the shish-kabobs that I make with uncooked spaghetti noodles and skewered raisins. I've placed these discretely in one of our kitchen cabinets for such a time. For Katie, she now has to make her own lunch instead of buying it, since she's not getting any lunch money from Mom. Dinner results in whatever is left in the freezer, carrying our name of Freezer

Food. With that name we're not really sure what it is that Mom is cooking until it's cooked and served. Sometimes this reminds me of the mystery meat served at Barrow Elementary, where I don't know what it is or if I'll even like it until I take my first bite. Nevertheless, we always have our roof over our heads, and something to eat.

With us moving or leaving Hope Avenue, it isn't too hard. For big changes such as this, Mom times it perfectly. The move takes place when we're at Daddy's for the summer. When we leave Mom in June, we live on Hope Avenue. When we come home in July, we live two streets over on Milledge Heights. Even more, it's a school move for me, too, going from the fifth grade at Barrow Elementary to sixth grade at Clarke Middle. Once again, I'm following Katie. She's going from the seventh grade to the eighth grade. My biggest point is the move to our new home that Mom bought.

In the *American Heritage Dictionary*, the second definition for *fight* states, "To quarrel: argue." From personal testimony, I know how this definition fits and holds true. I live with the application of this definition every day. I see it, I hear it, and I watch it, as the actions between my own mom and sister Katie display it. I'm not sure why. Sometimes I wonder if it's the similarities in their personalities, or it's because they are exactly the opposite. Whichever one it is, I do know that it's a daily power struggle with Katie against Mom, every day…and I mean every *single* day. Either way, it's a challenge or clash for the control of our house.

Greek and Roman mythology explains a lot for human society during that particular period of time. A thunderstorm is happening because Zeus is mad at one of his wives. There's a tsunami since Poseidon released the kraken for vengeful dominance of the people in the city nearby. With their lack of knowledge in the sciences of nature, isn't it perfect rationalization to only blame it on the gods?

In our more recent time period, Sigmund Freud justifies one of his psychology reasonings based on one of these Greek myths. This takes place when Oedipus kills his father, Laius, for greater attention and love for his mother. Freud identifies this specific behavior as the Oedipus complex, when the eldest son is going against or challenging their dad, but not necessarily killing him as Oedipus did. In short, Freud's Oedipus complex has this eldest son wanting and gaining power and control of the house.

Peggy Kohlmeyer

OK, that might make sense, but for us, Katie and me, as daughters instead of sons? Here Freud swaps us to the different myth of Agamemnon, who is away fighting in a Trojan war, and his wife, Clytemnestra, is having an affair with Aegisthus. Together these two plans to kill the father, Agamemnon, when he returns. The daughter, Electra, for the love of her father kills her mom. Since we're girls, it's Katie as the eldest daughter challenging the role of the mom, meeting and fulfilling the characteristics of the Electra complex.

Daily, Katie destroys Mom. Somehow, she's seeking the love of Daddy. This is a totally pointless battle since he's not even around for her to win his favor. The Electra in Katie is daily demonstrated by challenging or going against Mom. Katie won't even allow Mom to finish the final word of any of her sentences. Forget about her following any decision

Mom makes. Mom tries her hardest not to give in. Their fighting is instigated over anything and everything. Sometimes Mom has to be a mom and step in and say no to some of the "That's out of the question" things Katie asks. Not liking the answer, Katie pulls that additional tantrum, testing Mom, seeing if she'll eventually get her way or win. Unfortunately for Mom, the outcome is always the same. For every losing battle, Katie gives Mom her ultimate threat, "Well, I'm just going to live with Daddy." And the Electra in Katie creeps in.

These daily declarations made by Katie to Mom are constantly twisting a knife in Mom's side. A knife that Katie always seems to carry. For Mom, if she were to ever totally lose a fight with Katie and custody, it means that Daddy has won. Even more? It would mark him as a success and Mom as a failure in raising her own two kids.

Peggy Kohlmeyer

A loser is not our mom. She's had many hurdles in her own life, yet she's made the best of it for us. Daily she struggles, raising two daughters as a single parent and puts our needs and welfare first. Looking at what Mom has achieved, professionally she's set the example for us both to follow. I congratulate her on her own selfless acts. More than that, I also applaud Mom on her patience in dealing with Katie's never-ending threats.

Rebellion is in full stride for Katie, since she's a junior in high school going to Clarke Central, or in her eleventh-grade year. Following in her footsteps, I'm the new one still two years behind her, or in the ninth grade. Going to the same school, we don't look like sisters, and we don't act like sisters. The student body at Clarke Central is close to twenty-two hundred kids, so it's easy for me to be missed. While I'm still trying to find a circle of peers in my classes like geometry and debating in English class who actually killed the mockingbird, Katie has her own set of friends, since academically she's at the top of her class. Even though physically I shot up my eighth-grade year to five feet, ten inches and tower over her five feet, seven inches height, we're nothing alike.

This school year, Katie's earned a spot on the Clarke Central drill team. Here the squad perform during the high school football games. Busy? She's also got a part-time job. Mom did the duty of carpooling and transportation, but when Katie got old enough to get her license to drive, she had the perfect ammunition to cry out the need for her own car. Listening and supporting her independence, Daddy stepped in with this purchase, and now she feels that no rules at home apply.

Peggy Kohlmeyer

It's a normal Saturday morning and the day for our weekly chores. Katie's in her normal pose, sitting on the living room floor, leaning her back against the sofa. Katie's eyes are almost glued to the TV. Mom as always just wants us to pick up after ourselves. Hearing her voice reminding us, she's indirectly referring to Katie and her breakfast dishes. Glaringly, she looks up at Mom as if the most important moment of her life has been interrupted or as if she's been asked to move to the death chamber. "You don't have to remind us."

Even though it's eleven o'clock, and Katie's cereal bowl and spoon have been beside her since eight. Yes, Mom's made a simple request, and Katie's response begins today's clash. With Katie marking her control and challenging Mom's authority and simple request, she gets up and leaves the living room. Returning to resume her throne, she still hasn't put her cereal bowl in the kitchen sink.

The animosity and tension carry over into the afternoon. With the weekly chores still waiting to be done, it's now way past the time of breakfast or brunch. I've already finished cleaning the bathroom and vacuuming the floors. But still sitting in the same spot in front of the TV, Katie's only got to mop the kitchen floor and take out the trash.

Beginning her weekly debate, Katie understands and supports how I've got to clean the bathroom, since we all use it every day. She agrees that it does get dirty. She also understands that she needs to take out the trash, especially since it's in the kitchen and it's full.

What she doesn't see or understand is the need for her to mop the kitchen floor. Her argument is that it should be Mom's responsibility since she cooks dinner there for us every night. Why should she have to do it? It should be Mom's job. Also, she has to mop at work; why should she have to do it again at home?

As time continually elapses, breakfast is only a memory, lunch has been and gone, and time is now merging into the afternoon. The bowl from Katie's breakfast is still on the living room floor, and Katie's chores are still not done. The TV is on with the hum of some outdated afternoon movie. Asking the opening question to break the silence of communication in our house, Mom's curiosity is up, "What are your plans for the night?"

Katie sees this as her bartering line to get her way. It's almost like Katie's planned and prepared, saving for her defense. "I'll clean the kitchen if you let me go out with Cathy tonight." She's my sister Katie's accomplice but seemingly innocent friend.

With Mom not quick enough to answer, I only hear Katie shouting, "Even though I don't have to have your permission!" While Katie's finally up, taking out the trash.

Using the back door in the kitchen and walking to the outside trash cans on the side of our house, Katie automatically locks herself out. Making her choice of not using the shorter distance to get back inside with walking to the front door, I hear her tapping on the glass window panes of our back door for someone to let her back in. Why? I ask, since we all know that this back door has an automatic lock for safety.

Tap, tap, tap, I hear. Is she too plain lazy to walk around? *Tap, tap, tap*. I'm not wanting to give in to her, since I've had to listen to her complain and argue all day. She's made her choice of going to the only locked door in our house. After tapping on the door, she almost starts whacking. I'm just going to let her whack. Like everyone, she can walk around.

Tap, tap, tap. She's still knocking. *Tap, tap, tap.* Now it's like she's only knocking to piss me off. *Tap, tap, tap,* it's like she's expecting me as always to jump up for her. *Tap, tap, tap,* no one has come to her call. Instead she's still whacking on the door. I shout out, "Walk around!"

Tap, tap, tap. Maybe she's realizing now that I'm really trying to ignore her. *Tap, tap, tap.* Now not willing to admit to her own defeat, Katie still won't even walk around to the front. Instead she shouts out at me, "You better let me in!" With the underlying threat from her voice, her command is directed only at me. "You better let me in! Come unlock this damn door!" Demanding that someone get up and let her back inside. *Tap, tap,*

tap, I'm just tired of it all. Katie's constant hassles and demands.

Finally, with the back-door glass shattering, Katie totally wins this match. Hearing the breaking of this window and the sound of the glass hitting the back porch concrete floor, Mom and I are both running through the kitchen, almost colliding into each other. I see the middle window's been broken. Shards of glass lay all over the floor. Katie's standing with her fist halfway through what's left of our back-door window. Mom's grabbing the bath towel out of the dryer and wrapping it tightly around Katie's hand.

Standing back, I see the fragments of glass sticking from Katie's right fist. Katie's lips are quivering; she turns her head away, not looking down to see her own blood or the huge gash on her fist. Steadily, Mom picks the largest

Peggy Kohlmeyer

protruding pieces of glass out. "Peg, go get my purse and keys. We've got to go to the emergency room."

Katie's cut herself while placing an invisible knife deeper into Mom's side. Sneering toward Mom, "*Now* I'm going to go live with….!" Jumping in before she completes her ultimate jab, Mom simply and calmly replies, "I understand."

"*HIM*!" Katie blurts out. With our Mom finally, having to give in to the Electra in Katie's personality.

Chapter 9
Rocky Road

Daddy grew up in Mauk, Georgia. No, I'm not really sure where this city's name came from, but it's in Taylor County, a little to the left of the center of the state of Georgia. Connecting to history, Taylor County was named in 1852. It's named for our twelfth president, Zachary Taylor, not for him being our president but for his winning a victory in the Mexican War at Buena Vista. That's not the Buena Vista in Georgia by no means, with the pronunciation *Bue-Nah Vista* in separating the two. With all this history surrounding my dad, I knew he had to grow up to be something great as he did, especially making the two-mile trip to attend the nearest elementary school.

Daddy's mom married my grandfather when she was young. Waiting a few years to start a family proved that they didn't have to get married but wanted to get married out of love. At this time the Taylor County population had peaked at 11,473 residents. With this in mind, obtaining one's secondary education wasn't too important since it was also eliminating two working hands from any farm. Thinking of the time, this wasn't too out of the norm, and I think this is the reason my grandmother didn't get her high school diploma.

On the other side, my dad's father is someone everyone treats with respect. Grand Daddy is a self-made man with his tenacious spirit. Knowing the correct business decisions to make, he's purchased land when it's cheap. Holding on to it and knowing the time to sell caused him to become a nearby Houston County success. (Never fear, Texas, in Georgia it's correctly pronounced *House*-ton.)

His money being hard earned caused him to keep a tight rein on his wallet. Grand Daddy, not having continued or extended his own education, didn't want this to be the path for his kids. Knowing the times were changing, he made college tuition available for my dad.

Moving forward up to the time that Daddy's graduated from UGA, he joins the air force, fulfilling his medical license obligations. I've mentioned it before: Katie and I are only able to see him once a year. Remember, our full month takes place during the summer, since we aren't in school. This timing is not by his choice but negotiating the demand and difficulty in us getting there. It also pretty much marks our start of the "shared custody" in Mom and Dad's divorce. By plane or car, at the ages of three for me and five for Katie, our road trips begin.

Our visitation always goes through a step-by-step process. The first step is knowing where Daddy's military base is for that year. If we're staying with him at Keesler Air Force Base in Biloxi, Mississippi, the next question or step is how to get us there. Looking at a map, Mississippi is pretty much on the west side of Georgia.

This means we'll only have to hop over the state of Alabama. But driving all the way across that state in a car with two small girls can make it a very long drive.

To visit him at MacDill Air Force Base in Tampa, it's only a drop down the state of Georgia to the southern neighboring state of Florida. Traveling the interstate highway makes it a smooth ride. Getting us to Texas is a challenge itself. It's crossing Georgia to Alabama, to Mississippi, to Louisiana, and finally making it to Texas. With

Daddy at one of the five military bases in San Antonio, this is no doubt a plane ride for us to end up at Lackland Air Force Base. His last military base is back to Florida, at Eglin and near the town of Fort Walton. We're older, but this one's easier. It's his closest duty station yet.

On some of our visits, Mom and Daddy pick the halfway point, agreeing on their designated swap-off location. On other occasions, like him living in Texas, it's Daddy in his impressive air force military dress flying a round trip to pick us up. As we get older, Katie and I sometimes fly with airline supervision, or unaccompanied but with the guidance and watch of the airline staff.

Our visit happens around the middle of June to the middle of July. Legally, in the divorce agreement, he has full custody of us for this time period, but he's also obligated to have us for one holiday. The Fourth of July fulfills that legal requirement, too. This all changes, though, when he leaves the military.

After ten and a half years, he's served his country and paid his dues, and as we know, he's made the required military moves. As a former military doctor specializing in gastroenterology, he's the first of his kind to visit the city and establishes his practice in Columbus, Georgia. Now the custody arrangement changes, and we can see him for every holiday break.

It's only our first day in Columbus, with our spring break at school. Following Katie and Mom's falling out, Katie gets to the point asking Daddy about custodial rights. Almost rudely but directly Katie asks, "Daddy, now that you live in our state, have your legal custodial rights changed?"

Seeing Daddy's, a little shocked through his facial expression, but his interest piqued, the seriousness of her question is addressed when he replies, "Katie, let's discuss this tomorrow at my office."

At his office? We're meeting Daddy at his office? His location choice sets the precedence for our conversation.

"Katie, yesterday you asked me about any change in custodial rights since I'm now living in state." I'm hearing Daddy repeat this from yesterday to remind us both why we are here today. Right now at this moment, with this one statement, I'm realizing this is not about us. It's not about me. I see the seriousness of this topic since it's taking place in Daddy's office. It's about Katie. This is Katie's time to talk. My ears are only here to hear and my eyes to witness. I have no voice.

Peggy Kohlmeyer

Katie's right hand is under the table, this covers the bandage protecting the seventeen stitches she's received after smashing it through our back-door window back at home. Quietly, she begins, "It was completely dark, and it was late, and Mom forced us to sit outside on the front lawn." Katie starts out on one of her biased outcries of her episodes in living with Mom.

"Was this for punishment?"

"I guess so, I mean, I don't know. I just didn't want to sit outside. I can't believe she had to wake me up, too," Katie tells Daddy.

Instantly flashing back, I'm remembering this specific night when Mom sets her alarm, waking herself and us up. Getting us out of bed, Mom's using a flashlight to guide us in the dark to the center of our front yard, placing a blanket on the grass for us to sit. I understood her importance for this event. She wanted us to see the lunar eclipse. Sure, Mom wanted to see it, too, but more than that, for us all to watch it together. This was a lunar eclipse that only takes place once every fifty years. Katie's not sharing that part but goes on, "There were also times when we were younger that we had nothing to eat. I mean nothing."

"So, you would have to go hungry and miss meals?" Katie is questioned next.

"Yes, I guess so," Katie timidly responds, now not looking up, knowing she's lying but keeping her eyes down, focused only at the table. She knows that I know that she's lying, and if she looks at me, even a glance of my eye, she's afraid that she'll get caught. Now it's clearer. She's bad-mouthing our mom. I'm beginning to understand that Katie wants to make Columbus, Georgia, her permanent home.

Peggy Kohlmeyer

Biting my tongue, I'm really, really trying to keep my mouth shut. Mentally, I'm playing back the nights Mom's just dead tired. She's been at work at her school, adding onto that she's also had to make her drive, her daily commute. The nights that Mom's too afraid to sit down. She jokingly says, "I might not have the energy to get back up," but Mom always feeds us. There is always something for us to eat. She makes it her point to fix us dinner every single night, not knowing what we've eaten at school during the day.

Yes, this is also how Mom and Katie can start their fights, with Mom not meeting Katie's expectations for dinner. Since Mom's paid only once a month, by the end of the month when there's little money left in the bank, Katie always argues that "There's nothing to eat!" Dinner for Katie is something she wants to eat, not what she needs to eat.

Dinners that Mom makes have to have a meat and two vegetables. What does she mean, "No food?" How truthful does she think her words are? Aren't I proof enough of her lie? I'm the evidence that challenges her with her statement of nothing to eat at our house, when I'm an easy thirty to thirty-five pounds overweight, and Katie's new friend Lewis named me "Tank."

Not quick enough to answer, and what must have been after some thought, Daddy says, "Katie, I can't only take one of you. Peg, it's up to you to decide."

I can't even begin to imagine my life without Mom and what her life would be like without us, or at least me. This would mean living life in the opposite, seeing Mom only on the

Peggy Kohlmeyer

holidays and Daddy every day. Halting my thoughts, I feel Katie's eyes penetrating me. Feeling that she's only thinking about herself, rather than the best for both of us, my bottom lip quivers as I slowly start crying with a tear sliding down my right check. She's glaring at me, daring me to say no.

Not waiting for me to give the wrong response, Katie gives her reply, jumping up, "Oh, Daddy, you're getting the two-for-one special." Giggling at her own joke, Katie's claiming herself as the leader, deciding for us both.

Me? Am I just too pathetic toward her to even answer? Just as quickly, it seems the coin flips, and the animosity inside me sets. It's like I'm beginning to burn inside. *What*? I'm asking myself. Does she only, always, think of herself? What about my life? What about me at school? What about the things I've done? What about the things that I want to do? She forgets that I've made the Clarke Central basketball cheerleading team. She forgets about David, my boyfriend that I've dated most of my freshman year. She forgets that I really like my friends, Shelley and John, Augusta, Mia, and Mary. Some of them are friends I've known since Barrow Elementary and Clarke Middle. No, nothing about *me* is even acknowledged or addressed. It's only what she wants.

Suddenly I'm hit with my realization that I'm not cared about as a person. That I don't really count. Katie is the limelight child or the golden child who can do no wrong. What Katie wants and says goes for the both of us. She's the deciding factor for our immediate future. She's in full control. It's going to be the same thing, but instead of Mom, it's Dad.

Peggy Kohlmeyer

Connecting to Greek and Roman myths again, the Electra in Katie's personality is successful for another time. She's going to get her reward of what she wants. Again, maybe like the Roman population, I'm without a voice or any independence. Aren't I always used as her pawn? How is it possible to hate your own sister who you're supposed to love?

This June is the last time we go to visit Daddy since we are making a permanent move to live with him. Now things are pretty much reversed. I'll even call them the opposite since we're now going to be living with Daddy for the entire year. Opposite in that we also see Mom only on the holidays. For me that is just plain whack, I mean, completely out of the norm. Katie isn't making any effort to see Mom even when we're supposed to. When asked if she wants to go for a visit, Katie simply shakes her head no. I know Katie's sixteen now, but her choice even legal?

I ask myself what happened to name originality when Brookstone School matches our neighborhood's name of Brookstone. The private school across the street is only a three-block walk but crossing Bradley Park Drive without a crossing walk at a traffic light means we have to ride in a car. At this private school in Columbus, Georgia, it's the car that you drive as a student that's just as important as your family name. Your car is the status symbol that represents your father, his profession, or your entitlement. Fortunately, Katie and I don't yet rank, since we fall into the "newbie" group, as new students to the school.

Living with Daddy, Katie and I now have a living allowance. Yes, an allowance to live or money to cover our monthly expenses. Daddy's

Peggy Kohlmeyer

idea is that this is for us to budget our own expenses while not bothering and asking him, again and again. This allowance also includes us budgeting for clothing every month. At first this puzzles me. With Mom, we got back to school clothes at the beginning of the school year, but after that and especially for me, it was waiting until Christmas, a specific school event, or the infamous hand-me-downs from Katie that were never my taste, were too small, or never fit. Now it's new clothes every month. With cash to spend, how can I argue?

At Brookstone, as I mentioned, Katie and I are like every other kid that attends. Each child is an endorsement, or advertisement, of their parents. Not initially knowing of this, Katie and I enter the east wing of the Brookstone upper school building. On the first day of school, Katie and I are checked out as to what we're wearing, even down to the brand of shoes that we have on! Here, the cost of the child's clothes also represents the success of their parents. The more expensive the kid's clothing and shoes, the wealthier the family. Fortunately, it seems that Katie and I pass this initial test of knowing how to dress. Yes, I'll fully appreciate Daddy's idea of a budget with our new lifestyle.

In addition to our living allowance every month, Katie and I also get a weekly allowance. This allowance covers anything that we need to buy that week. Not the lunch at school, since it's already covered in the tuition, or the textbooks, since tuition also covers that, or school supplies, since that's set through a school charge account. Our weekly allowance is set to cover anything else. As a tenth grader, I ask myself, what else is there to purchase?

Establishing a routine in one to two weeks, I now really look forward to Fridays. Yes, it's the end of the school week marking it blue jean or dress down day at Brookstone School, which every student loves, but just as much, we get our weekly allowance. With movies, mall time, food out, or simply socializing with friends, I am financially strapped by Wednesday. Again, I credit my dad as being right, we do need that weekly allowance, too.

Living with Daddy is so different than living with Mom. Katie classifies this as her "lush life," one that we've both never had. For Katie, everything always has a price. By living with Daddy, we're going to a private school. This school is so close we should walk, but we don't since people would talk. Don't get me wrong, life with Mom for me was totally fantastic. Mom made sure we had the roof over our heads and that all our needs were met, although she only gave us the basics. A clothing allowance like Daddy's gives us what was not possible before. Instead, Mom provided Katie and me with the luxuries we took for granted that money can never buy: trust, love, support, and understanding. In hindsight, with Mom earning a beginning teacher's salary and Daddy's child support, I realize now in comparison the monetary struggles she had in raising two kids keeping her financially strapped. It seems to me that Katie is having her year of success and that this is all in Katie's plan of thinking only of herself.

For the following year, Katie's going back to Athens and attend UGA for her undergraduate degree. This is what I call an opportunity of our lifetime. What makes it so good? Daddy's paying for everything. The allowance that we have now is included but upped or increased for her with the additional expense of college tuition, textbooks, room, and board. Maybe he's reflecting back on his own college days, or maybe since we're girls,

regardless of what he thinks or his rationale, we're

plain fortunate to be his kids. This or his kindness

I'm calling the Pike Scholarship, based on our last

name. An all-expense-paid experience for earning

our four-year undergraduate degrees, meaning we

have to meet and maintain Daddy's expectations. If

Daddy had supported Mom in dealing with Katie

behavior, financially he would have gotten out a lot

cheaper.

Back in Athens, or what I'll always consider

home, Mom's got some adjustments to make. Her

dad or my Poder is off following his graduate

students to the Congo. Exotic and almost surreal,

both he and Mimi are there. Poder's contract or

agreement with the university has them away for two

years. As the university's professor in agricultural

economics, he's helping his foreign exchange

students wrap up their theses. His opportunity to live abroad for two years allows him to retire when he gets back, meaning he gets to retire three years early. My concern is about Mom. Now she's really alone in Athens with Mimi and Poder also gone.

Almost weekly if not more with a phone call, I update Mom, checking on her and addressing my concerns. In return she's always asking me about my school, my new friends, and if I've found anyplace to take ballet again. Switching the topic back to her, I ask her what she thinks about Mimi and Poder leaving. Mom had to move into the Tivoli Apartments and rent our house without the additional support of Daddy's monthly check. I hear the smile spread across her face as her voice picks up in her new, cramped space. She thinks it's the best idea for them, working and traveling abroad. I even hear a hint of envy. "Remember, I spent some time in Cambodia as a child when Poder was also working with some students then." She turns the conversation back to me, asking, "So how is it with your new friends? Tracy? Robyn?"

Filling her in: "Tracy has more sweaters than I've ever seen, with a closet just for them! Robyn? Oh Mom, she's so smart. It's like she doesn't even have to study. She beats me every week on every vocabulary test."

Now that I've eased up on my end of our conversation, Mom goes back to Mimi and Poder working abroad. "So, Peggy, what do you think? Would you like to live over there, too?"

What? I'm asking myself, "What did she just ask? Didn't she just ask me about actually living over there? What's she getting to?"

"Mom, what do you mean?"

"Well, with you girls living with your dad, and Mimi and Poder out of town and me in Athens now by myself, I applied for a job there myself."

"Mom, what are you talking about? Africa? You? You're moving to Africa, too?"

"Yes, but no. It's not with the university but with the International Schools. They have a position available, and they've been placing teachers overseas for years."

"I don't understand. If you're not with the University of Georgia, where will you live? I mean, how will you survive?" Asking her, creating a picture in my mind of my mom wearing a grass skirt, trying to survive in a jungle.

"No, no, no, Peg, you have it all wrong. It's a compound or a camp. I mean, an enclosed area, and it will be in the same area with your Mimi and Poder."

Peggy Kohlmeyer

With Mom's life no longer on hold for us, without having us to raise, this is an opportunity for her. This is the answer for Mom's long wait for her life to pick up again.

"Do you want to go?" Mom asks me, even though we've been living with Daddy for not yet a year. She starts listing the perks of travel and the flairs of an international lifestyle, "Oh Peg, first up you've got to get your passport! Then a direct flight to London, then Kenya, and arriving to a US-protected school at the Congo." She continues that once we're there, we'll continue to visit surrounding areas and countries during the school breaks. With my agreement, all I have to do is attend the school where Mom is teaching.

"What about Katie?" Thinking of her starting her freshman year at Georgia the following year.

"Oh of course. She'll just have to put her college on hold for a year, but this is an experience that only comes once in a lifetime."

"Wow," is my automatic answer in awe. Although I'm not thinking of any of the negative possibilities holding up my own future.

Handing the phone to Katie, it's her turn to talk to our mom. Listening in on their conversation, it's always so short. When I hear Katie give a quick "No", along with her raised eyebrow and sarcastic look of *Are you crazy?* I realize Katie's also been given Mom's invitation.

This is it. This is Katie. This is her only answer without any thought in regard to Mom's remarkable invitation. No other concerns, no other questions of Mom and how she is or where she's going. Just no. On the other end of the phone, from Mom, I can hear how her side of the conversation continues. She's going over the same details to Katie that she gave to me but with some extras. Now she's mentioning how this job is her opportunity as a good career move, building up her resume. Looking at Katie, I can't tell if Mom's still trying to persuade Katie or just fill her in on her decision, but I'm reading Katie's expression of complete disinterest, disconnect…and her levelheadedness.

Shaking my head in disbelief, I'm forced to focus on what's taking place after all these years. In this one specific incident, with this one specific answer, Katie's making it completely clear. For me I've figured out who she really is and what makes her tick: *Katie.* It's always got to be Katie. Only and always, she's got to be at the top of her own and everybody's list. Even with our mom leaving the country? Reading the expression on Katie's face, she doesn't seem to even care.

With Katie looking down at the floor, not having the guts to look at me, I rescue the phone from the cradle of her hand. I'm at a loss of words. What do I say to my mom to follow up to that? I'm thinking of all the good points I can express to Mom, that she'll have the freedom that she didn't have for her twelve years as a single parent, and this is an opportunity for her to think about herself. Everything is sounding good to me until Mom brings up her invitation again, "Peg, you can still go."

I know what I want to say, and my answer is no, but nowhere near the reasons that Katie has expressed. For me I'm trying to find out who I am at a new school, with new friends who value the importance of school and having an education. With all this, I can't burden Mom. Instead, with my own remorseful answer, I can only tell her, "Mom, I just can't go, I mean, I don't know what I want to do,"

Peggy Kohlmeyer

because I'm just too scared to tell her that I'm

beginning to really like the opportunities of my new

home.

Chapter 10
Foreshadowing

Brookstone Preparatory Academy in name itself reeks of money. The school was founded in 1951 with the school's mission statement, which reads *Brookstone School, a college preparatory school founded in the Judeo-Christian ethic and committed to academic excellence, endeavors to build in its students the core values of loyalty, courage, wisdom, honor, service, respect, and leadership.* The front lobby or loggia welcomes every individual the same way, with an ominous, hand-painted mural representing a cougar's head on the left-hand side. *Cougar Pride* encompasses the right-hand side, reminding you of what each student represents. Lockers are located outside each classroom. Looking at each one, you'll see that it's a locker, but without the lock. The school's

Peggy Kohlmeyer

handbook also includes that *Brookstone builds the character traits that will enable its students to take that personal responsibility, be that lifelong learner, and engage in meaningful service. Loyalty, courage, wisdom, honor, service, respect, and leadership are the seven foundational personal traits that Brookstone strives to build in its students.* Without locks on these lockers, this is a test of integrity for each student every day. Entering the upper school or high school, a sense of pride exudes with the cougar as the school's mascot, embellished with the colors of blue and white.

Hearing the students walk softly down each hallway is due to the carpet covering the school's hallway floors. Sitting on this carpet beneath the overhead skylights and beside the floor-to-ceiling windows, collective students socialize, flirt, and yes sometimes even study. When the school bell rings, this designates the morning break is ending and now panic time to make it to class in the designated three minutes.

Almost automatically, a warmth spreads over me entering Coach Youngblood's class. The sun's heat spreads through the classroom into a summer sweat, even with the air conditioning running in early March. As my English teacher, Coach Youngblood routinely attempts to balance his golf club on the tip of his finger; when his face breaks into a gracious smile, all hesitation for what's expected from us today begins. This is his distraction to alleviate our ultimate stress. Finishing the novel, *A Tale of Two Cities*, we all know that some outlandish assignment will follow as the culminating event.

Peggy Kohlmeyer

"Foreshadowing. What do you know of it? Anyone with a hand up to contribute?" Coach Youngblood breaks the ice, welcoming and acknowledging us, his second period class.

Quickly darting her hand up to be recognized, Robyn gives her answer of knowledge from a dictionary she probably read last night, "To give a suggestion of something that has not yet happened but will happen in the future."

"Of course, Robyn, you are definitely correct." How does she do that? I mean, she's the same age as me, the same grade as me, but how is she seemingly so much smarter than me? Daily in my own wonderment, I know she's the one in Youngblood's class to break the ice with her answering the first question. Robyn has opened today's topic.

"Now, who can connect that to real life?"
Looking around, Youngblood's new question causes
the puzzling look crossing many faces. Eyes rolling
up, kids shifting in their seats, thoughts are
processing, and connections are trying to be made.
Tracy and I make eye contact, daring the other to
answer. "What event can happen today that gives a
prediction of what will happen in the future?" Coach
Youngblood rewords his previous question.

Without raising his hand but blurting out, "If
I don't study for your vocabulary test on Friday, I'm
going to fail," Warren the Cougar quarterback
shouts out with the classroom chuckles resonating
throughout.

"Ah, Warren, good try, but wouldn't that be
more of common sense?" with more murmuring
and their snickering now heard. I mean, after all, he
is the school's quarterback. "Good try though,

good try. Come on, guys, think about what Robyn

shared, and yes, along with Warren, what event

today can predict or foreshadow an event

tomorrow?"

Billy's hand shoots up as if his mental

light bulb goes off, "OK, I've got it. Football

this past fall season, Georgia against Auburn.

Everyone knew that Georgia was going to win."

"Nah, man, you couldn't have predicted

that game. That's what's so good when those

two plays."

"Guys OK, OK, let's get back to the

point...which is not the Georgia-Auburn game last

season, the next season, or the season after that,

but foreshadowing."

Looking around the class again and seeing all

the puzzled looks starting to creep back in, right

before the hemming and hawing takes over, Edwin

slowly raises his hand. Coach Youngblood grins with relief. "Yes, Edwin, go ahead."

"Well, what about a palm reader? You know, a fortune teller? Isn't that a type of foreshadowing? I mean, someone is looking at your palm, and they're telling you of what's going to happen in your future. Doesn't that fit into foreshadowing?"

"Hmm, Edwin, you've got me on that. I've never thought about a palm reader. Has anyone here ever done this or known someone who did? How did it turn out? I mean, with their fortune or prediction coming through?"

"Remember that Ouija board? My sister tried that on me."

"At the Columbus City Fair, they tried to predict my weight."

"Did they get it right?"

"Heck no, do you think I'm going to get on a scale in public for everyone to see?"

Coming back to Edwin, "My mom goes to this guy, maybe even calling him a crazy guy, in Buena Vista to have her palm read. She swears by it."

"Yeah, my sister went to him, too. This guy goes by Saint EOM. He thinks he's fancy with all the saint stuff, but it's only his initials: Eddie Owen Martin. He's read my sister's palm, and she broke up with her fiancé. She called off the wedding."

"Boy, I bet your parents were glad. He saved them a ton."

"Edwin, go on, how has that worked? For your mom and all, how does she know that his prediction works?"

"I'm not really sure, but she drives out there about once a month, so something must be right."

"OK class, here it is…" Youngblood's statement causes all of us to groan. "You are to write about a prediction, a premonition, an event that holds true, therefore resulting in foreshadowing."

"Easy enough. I'm taking the Georgia Dawgs this next season to beat Auburn."

"Nope, that's too easy, and that's based on some other event, which is not your *own* life event." Coach Youngblood continues, "Your assignment is something in your life. A situation or an event that happens that is a prediction of what is going to mark an outcome in your own life." He's writing on the board to signify its importance.

"Five paragraphs?" a classmate asks.

Youngblood replies, "Not that much. This is a free write, not an essay. You do need to have the introduction, telling the reader where we are and what's going on. The body with supporting details, which of course is going to be the foreshadowing of the entire event. And then your conclusion, or the event itself."

"Whew" is what I'm thinking.

"When is this due?"

"It took three weeks to read the book, and you guys have spring break coming up, so let's make it due in three weeks."

"Spring break? We have to work on this over spring break?"

"No Billy, that's not what I said. You have three weeks until it's due. Let spring break be the time for the events in your life to happen, see what happens, and then write about them."

"Oh, OK, that's pretty cool."

Spring break and the beach? Nope, not for me. Now I'm going to split my time between visiting Mom in Athens and working on my English assignment. Yes, since now it's the opposite. We live with Daddy during the school year, but any breaks or holidays and we go back to see Mom. Or rather, I see Mom. Katie's not even here. It's a simple trip, too. Daddy flies me up, and then when I go back, he's there at the Athens airport to fly me. With his permanent move to Columbus, he sold his fishing boat in Florida, and I say he traded it in for his plane. It's a neat hobby for him to go fly somewhere. He's picking me up tomorrow. This is the easiest trade-off yet.

Peggy Kohlmeyer

Now I can see why Katie didn't make this trip to visit Mom. Her apartment is small compared to our house in Five Points. Thankfully, she's only here temporarily since she's accepted the job in Africa. All this unpacking she's done, she'll have to pack it back up again and put it into storage when she leaves in June. I know that this time when I leave Athens, it's probably the last time I'll call Athens my home. I mean, no one in my family is going to be left here for me to know.

Athens the city is the same, but in the few months since we moved to Columbus, things or friends have changed. My friend Shelley's broken up with John, which I never thought would happen. Then I come back and find out Shelley's sister is now dating my old boyfriend David. A stab in my back? If so, I'm not sure who is to blame. It's me who moved.

The talk at Clarke Central, my former high school, now seems the same as social or only gossip. My friends at Brookstone talk about events that are happening in the outside world more than about people at the school. If I don't watch the evening news, I'm missing out on the current topic of morning discussion at Brookstone.

Wait a minute, could I possibly use this for that English assignment? How does this all fit? If my mom's moving, what foreshadowing does this have for me? How am I going to fit her life experience into the foreshadowing for my life? Thinking about this now since I've got to make an A on Youngblood's writing assignment. How are my life events shaping me?

Rather than me being at the beach where everyone else is fighting the sun and sand I've decided I need to make my own visit to Saint EOM at Pasaquan[1]. This is all in the timing for doing my paper. Remembering to give Edwin my credit since he mentioned him at school, I'll just drive out and visit. When he makes my prediction, I'll only have to wait and see how it turns out. With a forty-five-minute drive, I can wait for the next twenty-four hours or so and see what happens.

While it's originally known as Pea Ridge, the drive I'm making to visit Eddie Martin in Buena Vista, Georgia, isn't all that long. With Buena Vista translating into "good view," I'm taking this as a sign for my decision. Following Edwin's guidelines that he mentioned in Youngblood's class, I've started out early and plan to wait. There's no calling ahead for reservations or any way to make an appointment. I can only be present and wait, which I'm doing.

---

[1] https://pasaquan.columbusstate.edu

Looking around Eddie Martin's compound or ranch, I'm not scared; I'm only more in awe. Every inch of every foot of everything has something on it. He's sculpted something everywhere I look. On every part of anything that there is to see and touch. This guy by himself and with his own hands built or created acres of all kinds of buildings and monuments, which he's totally enclosed with a self-sculpted concrete fence. Not a concrete block fence, but one that he's also made, and even more. There are sculptures on each and every part of everything. And yes, I'm meaning *everything* from the fence to the door frames, his walls, and up on his ceilings: human profiles, crosses, flowers, bodies, and the sun. It's all beautiful and breathtaking, but a little bit whacky, too. I mean, who could or would do all this?

Peggy Kohlmeyer

I wonder what message is he trying to send? It's like art but no way near the classic art styles of realism or impressionism. It's almost from another culture and a different era. Is this an Indian art style maybe? It's so basic in its presentation. He's got that simple, straight line in the form or shape that anyone can draw but going to the extreme that he's done it?

Thankfully, I'm easily distracted from what I'm about to do. Since the sun's fully out without a single cloud in the Georgia sky, I'm feeling a little more at ease. There's no way that I could have come out here if it were rainy or overcast. I mean, that would've made it that much creepier for me, since I came out here all by myself. Who's going to believe me? Now I've really got to meet this guy, if only for some type of evidence.

Waiting in his house in this front room, it's not that I'm bored when there's so much to see. With my time passing from ten to twelve, it's been a two-hour wait. Maybe that's why this Eddie guy's painted everything up. Only three, two, one more person to go in front of me, and then it's my time. "You! You're next." Saint EOM's assistant points to me. Looking up toward him, my total anxiety creeps in. What's this Eddie or Saint EOM going to say? What's his prediction for my life going to be?

"Come on, miss, this way."

I follow the tall, thin assistant as he goes down the two steps. He's walking so fast that visually I can't get everything in. All the art decorations from outside continue inside. Everything continues in the same bold, sharp, colors. Quickly, with the rush of our pace, I'm looking everywhere, my head turning right, then

Peggy Kohlmeyer

left, and back again. I'm trying to take in everything there is to see. I'm losing my breath trying to keep up with him as I express, "Please wait."

Finally, we're at the back of the house. We've almost sprinted through the length of the entire place making it to the back door. Stepping down the first back door step, looking up, there is more. More images, more murals, even out in this backyard. Stepping down the last doorstep, I look up. There he is *Saint EOM*, but now seeing him almost with a feeling of disappointment, he's not much at all.

Saint EOM sitting down doesn't give me the sense of fear that I've prepared myself for. He's just a man. An older man with a beard and gaudy or extravagant clothing in both color and style. Clean enough, even though he's outlandishly dressed. His assistant is still by my side. With him pointing to the folding chair placed across from Saint EOM, I take a seat. The assistant backs away, but I'm not turning around and following him to see where he's gone. I'm too worried to take my eyes off this Eddie Martin in front of me, or the one who goes by the name of Saint EOM.

Now with the two of us looking at each other, I'm too hesitant to speak. How does this go? Who speaks first? What's the correct so-called protocol? I mean, do I introduce myself first and give my name and such, or does he?

Tilting his head back, peering at me like he's got reading glasses on but doesn't, Saint EOM eyes me over, looking down the bridge of his nose. It's as if he's checking me out. Maybe to see how I'm made. Instantly, we're both thrown off, as a cool Georgia breeze comes through. Feeling the chills going down my spine I'm startled with a slight

Peggy Kohlmeyer

jump. It's a nice Georgia breeze. A spring breeze

that's not too cool and not too hot, without factoring

in the upcoming summer humidity. It reminds me of

the saying *When you feel the chill down your spine,*

someone has walked over your grave.

"I've got to have my palm read." In my

terse voice, I'm blurting out the reason for my

visit and letting him know that his keeping me

waiting really tested my patience. Eddie Martin

only nods. Following up, I say, "I've got to see if

your prediction is going to be true."

It seems that same Georgia breeze gently

tiptoes in again, reminding me that we're still sitting

outside. Yet this time, the breeze brings in an air

that causes some type of transformation to take

place. This same man is changing. He's now Saint

EOM intently eyeing me, tilting his head back for a

second time. "What do you want to know?" Saint EOM finally speaks.

Trying not to rush it all out, but with all the pent-up curiosity that I've had, "Well, I mean, what's going to happen to me?" Giving him a general question to respond to, hoping this is the way prediction and palm reading all starts.

Rather than his answer, instead it's a loud, sudden *thud* that we both hear. Quickly looking to my right with Saint EOM following my gaze and finding what caused the sound, a black crow lies completely sprawled dead on the ground. With mutual disbelief for what we're both seeing, Saint EOM simply shares, "I'm not sure if that message is for you or for me. Just make of it what you will." My eyes only lock with his, trying to understand his interpretation.

Peggy Kohlmeyer

Wow, call this one a slap. I'm taking a deep breath for what just happened. A crow, a black crow fell out of the sky dead. Looking up at the totally clear blue Georgia sky, I'm trying to make some connection of where this black crow came from and how did it just fall? Is it a prediction? Is it true? Is it for me or for Eddie Martin? Bringing my gaze back down to the seat in front of me, all I see now is his empty or vacant chair. I can only address this visit with a question of foreshadowing if it was for me or Saint EOM without looking into the palm of my hand.

Chapter 11
The UGA Warm-Up

Climbing the grade-level ladder of education, it's my eleventh grade or junior year at Brookstone High School. As always, Katie's still two years ahead of me, making her a freshman at the University of Georgia. For this year, I'm labeling it as my solo flight. For the very first time, Katie and I are apart. Growing up, we did spend the night away at friends' houses and went on Girl Scout camping weekends, but this is our first extended separation of more than a week. It's also putting a bigger separation between us in school. Katie is what some classify as "done," since she's finished high school, although she's stepping up and continuing her educational career going to the university.

Currently, the seniors at Brookstone are waiting on their acceptance letters from their prospective colleges, and juniors like me are just starting to get into the warm-up process of the applications and applying. When someone asks me, "Where are you going to school?" there's no hesitation in my reply with my quick, almost automatic response. "Back home." Reminding them "Athens, the University of Georgia." My worry isn't going home to Athens, but instead getting accepted to the university in the same town of Athens.

Wherever we've been, Katie's always taken the lead. She's set the example for me to follow of what to do, but just as importantly, on the opposite side of what not to do. Right here, right now, I don't have anyone else to follow and making up for her absence, I visit her every possible Georgia football weekend or home game. Yes, the Georgia football home games have me going back to Athens.

Remember, Georgia is where Daddy went to college, and he still supports the Dawgs. Establishing his residency in Columbus, he's taking the time to attend UGA games by flying to Athens. His single-engine Cessna, that is, that he flies on his own. When we were still living in Athens, Daddy had his own double dip: seeing Katie and me and getting in some football game time with the Georgia Dawgs. I've seen so many of these games played when I was a kid that visiting Katie for them is not all that special. Thanks to Daddy, I already know how to cheer for the Dawgs, and now on these weekends trips to see Katie, I'm fitting right in with the rest of the UGA fans.

My first visit is exciting, seeing Katie and her dorm life and her living on her own. But with every visit, afterward it ends with regret. It's not because I'm regretting my return to the town of Columbus where my daddy lives. It's not regretting returning to my high school life after the UGA victory homecoming game against Vanderbilt, all the while missing my own at Brookstone School. It's only this time, with every movement, the dread is in every step I take. I regret when I realize I'm leaving my sister, Katie, again.

Suddenly, like a snap, a bright idea is popping into my brain. What if I didn't have to make a return trip after my weekend visits? What if I'm already living in Athens as a college student? What if Katie and I are both living here? First, I've got to see how to apply.

The University of Georgia college handbook quickly becomes my best friend or lifeline. I'm actually reading, really reading it, every single page.

In addition to my school work for my junior year, I've also added my new hobby: UGA acceptance. My diligence is rewarded when I find the information located on page fifty-seven. This information is still in the general introduction section that people usually breeze over, so I see why no one notices it or one of the Brookstone School counselors hasn't pointed it out to me. Here it says, in this "magic box," the list of the class requirements for acceptance to the university.

Looking over this list for the required courses for consideration for UGA acceptance, it's showing: Four English classes, three math classes, three science classes, three social studies classes, and two years of foreign language. Taking in the logistics or simple math, it's the four English classes that will take four years. Having only one English class each year is the hurdle that's tripping up many students since, by their junior year, they only have three classes and have to wait until twelfth grade to get that last English class.

Mentally checking it off, I've got the three for math, the three for science and the three for social studies, earning the needed credit for each one of my ninth-, tenth-, and eleventh-grade years. For English, it's the same with one class for ninth grade, tenth grade, and eleventh grade, but since I'm also taking Greek and Roman vocabulary, covering the stems and prefixes, I'm set. This class qualifies as an English class, therefore meeting the requirement for English class number four. *Holy smoke*! Following the listed course requirements, I've met every high school course qualification needed or required for UGA acceptance.

My next UGA acceptance requirement to meet is passing the SAT. And when I say passing, I mean the composite test scores of math and English having to be high enough for me to qualify on the Georgia acceptance list. Remembering back to the actual morning of the test, I'm stressed thinking about taking the test, rather than the test itself. Now waiting on the test results is the total definition of stress. Sure, like other people I can retake or take the SAT again, but if I do, I'm missing the UGA deadline for acceptance for their upcoming school year. For me it's this one score that I'll earn that one morning that can determine my future.

This morning's discussion at Brookstone School are the scores that are finally out. Making this the translation for the SAT results that I've also secretly waited for. "Oh, did you hear what Joey got?" *Joey?* That slams my thought of them being mailed in alphabetical order with Joey's last name beginning with a *W* for Williams. How could this happen? I didn't get mine, jumping to the conclusion that they weren't sent this way, with my last name beginning with a *P*. Quickly, I'm thinking of some other connection or order, coming up with zip code. If I live in the 31904 area, his has to be in the 31901, 31902, or 31903 areas.

Listening back to the hallway conversation. "I wonder what his parents said." Not knowing his score but wondering if it's high enough for him to get into Vanderbilt, where he wants to go.

"You know, Cissie is going to get offered every scholarship with her score."

"And you know with their money, her SATs don't matter at all. That's what's odd about it."

"Can you believe Brian made a totally perfect score? I mean perfect. What's the chance of that?"

"He didn't miss one? Not one question?"

"Not a single question. Can you imagine getting every question right on both parts?"

Wow is what I'm thinking to myself. When my score only has to be is high enough to get me into UGA. But a perfect score, how did he do that?

"Nope, he didn't miss a single one, I mean a totally perfect score."

Hearing all the talk, I'm feeling like it's got to be my lucky day with my scores in the mailbox back home.

Walking down the driveway knowing the mail is here, I'm really only wondering if my SAT score is there. With my hesitation and one deep breath, lowering the mailbox door for today's mail, my test results aren't on top. One, two, three letters down after those addressed to Daddy, finding it,

it's here. I've gotten my score!

Not thinking about saving the envelope but

tearing it open at the back seal, I'm reading, I'm

reading, and I've not only passed, but my final

combined SAT score is high enough placing me in

the required top qualifying percent for UGA

acceptance. Putting the two together with me having

covered number one, meeting the high school class

requirements set by UGA, and number two, having

high enough SAT scores, can only equal number

three. Acceptance to the University of Georgia.

Now for my biggest task yet, which is number

four: getting Daddy's permission.

With me skipping forward since I've

completed steps one through three, it's still up to me.

Having the UGA acceptance letter, which I consider

full ammunition, I've got to somehow create the

persuasive argument to Daddy on why he should allow me to attend UGA. If this was a year later in my senior year, it would be an easy yes, with the additional benefit of in-state tuition. Now, though, how do I explain to him to let me go to Georgia when I'm not even out of high school and right now only sixteen years old and still in my junior year?

Gathering up my gumption the best way I know, without saying a word, I give Daddy my UGA acceptance letter. Opening it quickly, he replies, "Wow, Peg, this is great."

"Thanks, Daddy, but look at the date. It's for this upcoming year," I add, jumping in.

"What? Peg, I don't understand. Next year is for your senior year, your last year at Brookstone."

"Yes, Daddy, but I have all the required courses, so I went ahead and applied to Georgia. As you see, I got in."

With him intently looking at my acceptance letter again, or what I consider my winning lottery ticket, I begin with my persuasion. "Daddy, in addition to you not having to pay another year's tuition at Brookstone School, it's also another year with me not living at home and my allowance." Pausing at this time for him to really understand my request. "Just think of it all. I'll have a jump start at Georgia," continuing with my encouragement, "and with tuition going up every year in both places, Daddy, think of it." I pause and wait for the dollar signs to click for him. "If they didn't want me as a student, I wouldn't have been accepted." Which has to be true.

Not wanting to sound like I'm mumbling but continuing with my plea. "Daddy, it's not like I don't know where I'm going. I'm going back to Athens. I'm going back home." Looking at him as he continues reading my letter of acceptance, his eyes go back and forth from me to the letter, back to me. Raising his eyebrows as if he's really reading something of interest. I give him my last, saved piece of hope. "And Katie's already there."

Taking a minute more to ponder before asking me, "Peg, you did all this on your own?" Nodding my head silently in agreement, saying yes, I take this as his congratulations on my acceptance, but even more on my plan. Elation inside me erupts, hearing his golden words. "Peg, after all this, of course you can go."

Let me now mention Daddy's stipulations. In order for me to attend UGA in the fall, I first have to further prove myself and my academic ability by passing all my first semester classes at Columbus University's summer school! *Summer school*? My face momentarily freezes with the grin

I had with his initial yes, thinking of what he's making me do to make it to Georgia in the fall. Letting his message sink in. He's telling me I have to go to school this summer semester. *Summer school?*

When Daddy tells me of attending Columbus University for the summer, I smile, as I see it as my summer camp, while viewing it as another opportunity to get ahead. Summer school gives me the option to take the entry-level freshman classes: English composition (English 101), American history, and basic algebra. Having these three classes completed by fall semester, I'll start at UGA as second-semester freshman, putting me even further ahead of my peers.

Applying the expression "two for one" fits perfectly for me now. Especially since my junior year in high school is at the same time my senior year, or last year at Brookstone School. Thinking of what I'm missing out on next year as a senior is not really what I would consider much. I mean, I won't have to complete my senior exit project, which is on the side of good, but on the opposite side, I won't get to go on the senior trip. I also won't be around as a senior for the chance of a possible nomination to the homecoming court in the fall or attend Brookstone's junior/senior prom in the spring. With these as the highlights of my senior year, I'd say I'm not missing all that much.

With the school year coming to a close, I feel it's still too early to let my secret out. Leaving Brookstone School on the very last day, for my very last time, I think that I've got the biggest secret. With the hugs, shouts of "See you next year," and tears, I'm smiling and almost tickled inside. No, I haven't told anyone where I'm going for the following school year, or my plan of attending UGA, or that I won't see them when they all return in the fall. I still have not one, not two, but three major tasks at hand to accomplish this summer with the classes at Columbus State University that I have to pass. If I don't meet this different set of goals, I have the threat of returning to my same spot with this student body for the upcoming school year.

Also, this summer on my list, I have to decide on my college major. Daddy says if I'm so set to go to UGA, then I have to know what degree I'm going for. I have to have more of a decision than "undecided" as my student status. Narrowing the array of choices, I start with my own degree list of qualifications: No foreign language and no advanced-level math or science. My major also needs to be marketable and in relatively high demand. I mean, after four years, I want a job. Most of all, it needs to be a career that I will enjoy, but thinking of another must, it must be a relatively easy major for me. After using my summer camp semester to peruse the available majors and degrees, the one that fits me perfectly is fashion merchandising, since I love to shop.

Always having a plan and planning ahead, if I complete high school in three years, I also want to complete my college degree in less than four. Starting the University of Georgia at the age of sixteen and adding four years to that to earn my fashion merchandising degree, I'll be twenty when I graduate. By skipping my senior year, I'm now only one year behind Katie instead of two.

Also, it's understood that if Katie and I don't go to school for the summer, we have to go back and work in Daddy's office. This is part of the Pike Scholarship plan that Katie and I are both supposed to follow. If Daddy supports us, we're going to school. If we're not going to school, we have to find a job to support ourselves. I can't argue since this seems fair. I'm so fortunate to have him pay for school and not ever getting the attitude of entitlement. Going to school in the summer is actually better than I thought. I see that it's not so hard. In fact, it helps me stay focused to obtain my goal.

"What about your mom?" is a question that close friends often ask. Not to overlook her since she's not in Athens when I go back to start my freshman year. With the extension of her two-year overseas contract in Africa, the school is now paying for Mom's first visit home. Having Mom in Africa is difficult, but what can one expect when we are the ones who initially left her? Making up for the summer that she missed, Mom's promised Katie and me both a European vacation trip. The general itinerary proposed by Mom is for Katie and me to fly from Atlanta to London. Meeting Mom after two years, we'll have a lot of catching up, as well as recovering from jet lag. After our own three-day tour of London with the shops and shows, we'll join an American Express twenty-seven-day booked tour. Following the travel brochure, we'll leave London and visit France, Switzerland, Monaco, Italy, Austria, Germany, and Belgium, ending in the Netherlands. Mom's idea is to give us an introduction to Europe so that we can later follow up on our own.

Needless to say, to Mom's invitation Katie simply says no, using the excuse, "I need to go to summer school to get in some more classes." For me the trip from Mom is the utmost high school graduation present even if I didn't graduate. With

Katie out of the picture, I'll also have some time

with Mom to myself.

Chapter 12
The Final Semester

My degree title states home economics, but it's a title for my major that I feel doesn't exactly fit. There is no *home* in any part of my fashion merchandising major. The required courses to complete this degree vary from Retail Management Foundations to The Study of Clothing with History and Design, while also adding in the business aspects of marketing. This is all fine, but I question how it is part of home economics. Furthermore, having accounting courses, along with micro- and macroeconomics classes all qualifies in my mind more toward a business major. But it doesn't. Nevertheless, home economics is the degree I'm earning; with my last semester to go, I have no chance to argue. Plus, the way I look at it, I'm just buying clothes only on a larger scale, which I already love to do.

Finalizing my fashion merchandising degree with an internship is optional. For this internship, Daddy still has to pay the semester's tuition, while students work at the cooperating business to finish their degrees. New York, Miami, and Atlanta are areas that fellow classmates boast. Me? I'm interning at the Dillard's store back in Columbus, Georgia. I want to leave home but not fully yet, since I'm not completely ready to live in another city that I don't know. I'll even label myself a babe in the worldly woods at the age of twenty, since there are many things I still can't do. Yes, definitely I drive, and I vote, meeting those two with the ages of sixteen and eighteen, but I don't drink alcohol since legally I can't with the age set at twenty-one.

This semester at Georgia is my last semester. It's *so* going to work out for me without having academic stress. This semester, I don't have any core or academic classes. The only sit-down class I have to take is considered an elective class: Computer Science 101. I feel as though I've saved the best for last is in regard to the three physical education or PE classes to take. I planned it this way. I mean, maybe I've been holding out this entire time at UGA to break the sweat. Now I'll take them all in one semester, labeling it my summer of sweat.

My summer sweat schedule consists of tennis, athletic endurance, and bowling. Julie, my sorority sister and summer roommate, and I are getting into shape to complete the Peachtree Road Race. Did I plan it all this way? Well, having registered for three PE classes, I think can only help

Peggy Kohlmeyer

me finish that race. Anyway, the Peachtree is not until the Fourth of July.

Me participating in The Peachtree Road Race? OK, so Julie and I don't ever run, but with the training schedule we've both agreed to, Julie and I start out simply doing four laps on the UGA track, making it a mile. After that we'll only need to add lap after lap, adding up to 6.2 miles to complete this 10K race.

Actually, when we're at the UGA track after the first bend, we're both jogging and panting, and I'm losing Julie on the straightaway. Humbled, I finish our first lap solo, waiting and cheering Julie, "Come on, finish it! You've got it," until she ends, standing bent over next to me. This reality of our running ability only dampens our plan, while we're both calling it a night after a quarter of a mile.

Neither Julie nor I have been back to the track since our first attempt in April, but I'm feeling pretty sure my PE classes will get us there. Since today is only June 17, by July 4, I figure we can both labor through our first, and maybe only, 10K Peachtree Road Race.

The summer semester kicks off with its Monday classes starting on time. Not that this is unexpected or surprising, but there's been a huge heat wave that's baking the South. I mean, a real baking for college students walking to their classes when the eight o'clock morning temperature is eighty-three degrees and the relative humidity is 90 percent. Calling it the science of weather, it's already making it feel like ninety-two degrees and only at 8:00 a.m.

Walking up to the UGA tennis courts and seeing the note left by the coach, he's only asking us to sign our names showing our attendance. He further sates, "If the heat continues, we will meet Wednesday at Stegman Hall." Curious as to how it's possible to play tennis in the scorching heat, I'm now even more intrigued about playing tennis in the college gym. Signing my name and feeling disappointed, I'm also relieved, as I'm feeling the sweat running down the back of my neck.

OK so much for that 8:00 a.m. class. Next? A sweaty, casual walk down the hill into Stegman Hall for athletic endurance. I'm moving especially slowly, not only for the heat, but having some extra time to kill after my first class didn't really meet. Just entering Stegman gives me a comfortable feeling of familiarity. Going back to my childhood and our move to Athens after my parents' divorce, no question, no doubt at this point in my life, Athens is still my home. With this as the last day of my last quarter before I can graduate, I'm trying not to get upset. Who knows how many more times I'll have this same opportunity to carry out or continue what my grandparents started.

My grandparents initiated calling Athens home since my grandfather received an invitation to join the University of Georgia faculty. He's a positive influence for me to follow, both professionally and physically. Poder I'll forever idolize. Growing up on an orange farm in Sebring, Florida, he enlisted into the military directly out of high school. He filled his call to serve in the US Army during World War II. While serving, he completed his undergraduate degree and moved up in rank.

Finishing his military duty, landing in Okinawa, Japan, with the US Seventh Army, he attended Cornell University on the GI bill. At

Peggy Kohlmeyer

Cornell, having already married and had two kids,

he earned his master's and PhD. He earned them

both in four years. My point? Poder is now in his

upper sixties, and before he went to Africa to

follow his graduate students, daily he did a one-

mile swim here at Stegman Hall. Therefore, I stand

a little taller walking through the door, thinking of

him with my own sense of pride, wanting to live up

to what he can do.

Swimming? I'm not worried or rather not

really worried about this class. Confidence is key for

me, as swimming is the area that I know. I wasn't a

lifeguard during the summer or a camp counselor. I

know swimming because of a crush I had.

I had a crush on a guy named Steve. At the

time of this crush, Steve graduates UGA with a

business degree. He's also living in hot Atlanta.

Steve is not only cute but good looking and

working, which puts him ahead of me, so this really might be my envy. My crush for him quickly ends, like an abrupt stop, I mean a huge stop, when Steve says he can't even think of asking me out.

"Why?" I wonder so much asking him.

"Your thighs are too fat."

"Too fat?"

"Yes, too fat."

I'm five feet, ten inches and weigh 133. I wear a size six, or maybe even making that an eight. You know how sizes go, so if it's a small size eight, then a ten, but still Steve's saying my legs are too fat? Taking all of what he's saying to me to heart and as a sucker punch from him, too, I could've died. I mean, he's totally killing my ego. Instead, though, rising above all that, I give him my sweet, polite "Thank you."

Peggy Kohlmeyer

His comment is a devastating personal jab for me, but for every problem, there's some type of solution. His comment lets me know what others also might see. My answer? Fix it. At the Athens YMCA, I do what Poder did every day: swim one mile…and that was last year, before this summer's sweat class schedule. Boy, if Steve could only see how thin my thighs are now; I'd even shout out to him my double thanks for motivating me.

With the focus back on the people sitting on the gym benches here at Stegman, there are more guys than girls. The guys appear to be in shape, but four or five of the girls are like me. Not so much out of shape and not the thin but what some might call a healthy size. The coach is giving us that PE pep talk about meeting the responsibility of getting into shape for a better and longer life. I'm thinking about the immediate, the race. I only want to finish the Peachtree Road Race.

Next for my classes is my real class or calling it a non-sweat class, computer science, which doesn't meet until after lunch. I'm calling this class almost a gift in disguise because I've also lucked out with this as an afternoon class meeting inside. In the heat of the day, I'm listening to the hum of the computers running as my chill from the classroom air conditioner keeps everything cool.

My last class of the day is bowling. It isn't at the top of my list of favorite classes, but it's off campus and on my way home. Bowling is definitely not my forte, as evident with my first game score of a twenty-seven. Following game guidelines, the higher the score, the better the player. My bowling balls are only making it into the gutter of the lanes. That's OK; it's only my first game on the first day.

Peggy Kohlmeyer

The instructor suggests that for the next class, I pick

a lighter ball. Easily, I agree. That's it, my courses

for my last semester at UGA. Since it's a short

semester all in six weeks, I have everything every

day. Short, sweet, and intense with Athens, Georgia,

summer heat.

With my sister Katie changing her degree so

many times, I'm doing the opposite and staying

right on track. I don't think she's thoughtful in

regard to my dad. Sure, he's got two daughters, and

he's sending us to college, but that's just it. He's

sending us to college. It's been our all-expense paid

trip. It's Daddy's money that we're using. Because

of this, I'm staying focused on my degree with

respect to my dad. I've even helped Daddy out by

skipping my senior year in high school, creating my

own early-acceptance program. Daddy had his

qualifying conditions or stipulations with my first

semester at the local community college during the summer. With all As, I made it here for fall sorority rush. On the other side, Katie's changed her degree so many times, with so many different opportunities, it seems she's taken Daddy's financial support too far.

Picking my degree was easy. It consists of no foreign language and no advanced-level math or science classes. Math has given me headaches growing up. Mimi worked with Katie diligently to learn her multiplication tables and algebraic expressions. Katie is the golden child or shining star.

Sometimes I feel jilted or overlooked since Katie has the brains, and everyone knows one day she is going to be famous. I'm the one with the creativity, although I can't draw, only making straight lines and stick people for art class. In the musical aspect, other than ballet as a kid, the clarinet in the sixth-grade band is as far as I was able to get. So, I'm not even musically inclined. Again, this is when I stand on her sidelines cheering her on.

Katie and I are definitely opposites. As I mentioned, I see her as the golden child from the Asian tale. This is the one who is first born. The one who will have success. The child to whom all glory will come. Me? While not to call myself a mistake, but for us second born in the family, I'm the other child. Don't get me wrong. This is totally OK. While she's getting her praise and glory, I'm enjoying my life humming my own tune. I'm working twice as hard earning the praise Katie takes for granted. Katie treats people as though they owe her for her time, while I appreciate all the time you spend with me. Even when she makes her wrong choice or bad decision, I'm learning from her with the idea of what to do. I'm working toward making a positive impression, so when I walk into the room, people are glad that I'm there.

Except for the trip when I met Mom in Europe, I've been at summer school every summer to get ahead. This is my responsibility in keeping the Pike Scholarship plan, too. I can't argue. It seems fair. With me completing high school in three years and starting UGA at the age of sixteen, I'm now going to complete college in less than four. I'll graduate when I'm twenty. This quarter is closing in on what I consider a wonderful college experience.

My biggest lifelong goal is graduating on time. And with my goal so close, it's now shining brightly. This is my last semester of *de*-pendence. My next step is *in*-dependence. At the end of this semester, I'll have my full independence and responsibility for myself instead of me moving from

Peggy Kohlmeyer

one parent to another every summer or holiday. Finally, I'll have my own goals in life to achieve, rather than those set by my dad or mom and the university.

Working while going to school looks impressive on a resume. Working at a retail establishment in the area of my degree looks even better and gives me some of the experience that I need. With me always planning and taking the right path to achieve my goals, one of the pebbles in my path is my part-time job at the mall.

Casual Corner is a woman's clothing store. Casual Corner caters to the working woman with the "Buy Five and Have Fifteen" sales design. This marketing strategy encourages the customer to purchase one pair of pants, one skirt, two tops, and a blazer or sweater as the needed five ingredients to create the fifteen most outstanding outfits. As an employee, a one-item sale isn't enough, but multiple items in a sale increases the employee's sales score.

Brenda is a fantastic retail manager. With three full-time employees and then five part-time employees, four other college student girls and myself, there is never an argument about working hours. Twenty hours a week is easy to schedule, and extra hours are easy to pick up when one of the other girls needs time off. I enjoy working here with these people. The ladies and atmosphere are pleasant without any petty cat fights. There isn't any commission on what we sell, but sales competition and bragging rights for the best or strongest weekly sales are motivating forces.

On Saturdays, usually the busiest day of the week, the competition for multiple sales usually results in laughter. Sara, Jennifer, Michelle, Olivia, and I, as the sales associates, easily put an outfit of three pieces together for the customer or client.

Upping the count becomes our competition. Will

this customer buy the pant to create another outfit

and then increase our score? Or is it only a pair of

earrings or a necklace to close the sale? Olivia has

the swag with the multiple sales. Sure, a pant, a top,

but she doesn't forget the sash around the waist to

pull the two colors together, with the earrings and

necklace to perfectly match. Her customers know

her by name and even make appointments with her

when it's time for a new shipment to arrive. I'll

always have to compliment Olivia on this and copy

her finesse in customer service.

Thinking back to our phone call last night.

"Work for you tomorrow night? You bet! Olivia,

let me say thanks for calling me because

otherwise, I'm going to be bored." With my quick

shower and change into the proper Casual Corner

attire, I'm feeling that all this can only end greatly as my first day of my last semester at UGA.

Peggy Kohlmeyer

Chapter 13
Totally Clueless

Saint Francis Hospital in Columbus, Georgia, is a hospital I know. I know it since this is where my father sees his patients. My dad's office is in the neighboring physicians' complex. Today is totally different, though, since we're going out the front door of the hospital rather than us going out of Daddy's office door. This is different and out of the norm, but I guess we just came by to see Daddy during his lunch. Lunch? His lunch? That's weird. I've never been to Saint Francis Hospital to see Daddy for lunch.

"You guys wait here, and I'll go get the van," Daddy's saying. Van? Why did he say van? We only use the van to drive the distance to the University of Georgia football home games. Around town, if we go anywhere, we go in my stepmother Linda's white

SUV, so everyone can fit. Suddenly, puzzlement envelopes my mind again, seeing Daddy walking away.

Why is he going to get the van? Why are we here? The puzzlement in my mind continues into odd or even weird areas, as I'm fading in and out of reality. It's like a movie of my life is going on, but I'm stepping out, out of touch of where I am right now and everything that is going on around me. Pausing and waiting, as time passes I'm back in the picture or reconnecting and glancing out the hospital window, I notice how bright the sun is shining. It's so bright it's making me squint or close my eyes. Asking myself why this is so bright, then I wonder with curiosity why it is that I haven't even seen the sun in a while I mean, a long while. But I don't even know why. Even worse, I can't think of an answer to my

question of simply not seeing the sun. Just as
quickly, I'm suddenly reconnecting to my here
and now, remembering that I'm at the hospital
waiting for Daddy, squinting with the reminder of
the morning sun glaring into my eyes.

Morning sun? Did I just think that it's the
morning sun? If it's the morning sun, it's too early.
Too early, which means that we aren't here to eat
lunch with Daddy. I grin inside with this one simple
connection that I'm making, identifying the morning
sun rather than the afternoon sun. I feel a short burst
of success for my accomplishment of knowing this.
Just as quickly, I'm questioning why I'm happy with
being able to do something as modest as identifying
the time of day with the position of the sun.

As Daddy is pulling the van up under the
Saint Francis front door awning, I realize by making
the new connection that it's time for all of us to

leave. Tuning back into my own movie, I'm trying to stand and leave. Stand? Questioning myself: why am I sitting down? I've got to get up and follow everyone else outside. Why I am sitting down is the most important question that enters my mind. My sense of puzzlement and almost confusion returns, noticing that everyone else has been standing up. They're all standing up waiting for me.

Hearing "No, Peg, you stay seated until your father comes around," I recognize the statement that's directed to me by a lady in a white outfit. Now things are starting to get even more peculiar. White outfit? Hospital? Making this association, putting the two together, she's got to be a nurse. That's what she is, she's a nurse. I've identified her job with another sudden burst of my personal success. Continuing and focusing with this thought to almost categorize it as something I now know, I've successfully identified

that her job is the job of a nurse, and she works at
the hospital with my dad. My puzzlement returns,
since there is no association that I can make between
visiting Daddy at his hospital in the morning and
now this nurse. Just as much for me sitting at the
front lobby door of Saint Francis Hospital, since
that's where we are. My own frustration is beginning
since I am so confused. None of this is making any
sense to me.

Stay seated? The lady in white or the nurse
lady told me to stay seated. But why am I sitting in
the first place? This is a lobby where people go in
and out; they don't sit unless they're in a wheelchair.
With dread, I'm now glancing down at my arm rest.
That's what I'm sitting in, a wheelchair. This sudden
surprise hits me with shock, but also with a little hint
of anger. With defiance, I question in my mind, why

am I sitting in a wheelchair? Why am I leaving the hospital?

Looking to the van pulling up and seeing Daddy getting out, I'm trying to stand up again. This time the nurse, gently laying her hand on my shoulder, says "No, darlin', you just stay where you are," with her twang reminding me I'm definitely in the South.

Daddy, striding through the front sliding glass doors, emits his sense of assurance and strength that I need at this time.

Getting behind me, Daddy pushes me in the wheelchair outside toward the van. With the *whoosh* of the hospital sliding doors closing, the South Georgia heat envelops me. The months of June, July, August, and now early September are only a void to me. I have no connection or remembrance that these months have passed with no memory of them except leaving today. At the same time, I'm having a sudden blistering reminder that this is one of those dog days of summer, as the humidity and heat begin to make my skin feel sticky.

Searching again for that small, personal success and trying to connect the nurse's Southern drawl with the summer heat of Columbus, Georgia, I can't figure out how these two fit together. Most of all, why am I here? Finally admitting to myself I just don't understand what's going on. Why did we come here to visit Daddy at the hospital in the morning, in the heat? Why are we leaving? Even more, why am I the one sitting in a wheelchair? Daddy rolling me out pushes me to the opening of the van door.

With him bending over to lift me up, I quickly add, "No, no, Daddy, you're going to hurt your back," as he gives a deep heave, lifting me and my wheelchair up. Instantly, I'm struck with guilt.

Connecting everything I now know, I realize something has happened, and it's happened to me. I'm mean, he can't do that. My dad has the brains that can't be matched, but how can he even attempt to lift the combined weight of the wheelchair with my body, too? This idea is totally blowing me away. Now I understand that something is definitely wrong. I know my own weight, but with me in a wheelchair, the combined weight has got to be too heavy. Glancing at him he's looking the same. He's not hunched over with a hernia or such, but if he can lift what he just did, something is wrong. Only if something is *not* wrong with him, does this mean that there is something wrong with me?

While sitting in the back of the van, my mind is totally empty. There are no thoughts that I can go over. There is nothing that I can even ponder to think or try to recall. Desolation, a void, a totally open, empty, blank space is all I have in my memory

banks. Worst of all, I can't even answer my own

"Why?"

After pulling up onto the driveway and

parking, Daddy's picking me up again in the

wheelchair. This time it seems easier for him to

place me on the ground, rather than lifting me up as

he did into the van. I don't even hear a *humph* from

him.

We don't go through the garage and up the

two steps to the side door, but he rolls me on the

sidewalk around to the back of the house to the patio

with the sliding glass doors. Here is only an edge or

sliding-door railing, and Daddy now gives his final

humph, lifting the wheelchair and me up and over

into the back-bonus room.

Entering into the bonus room at the back of

the house, things look totally different. Originally, it

was the bonus room, with a pool table, TV, and a full bathroom. When we started living here, it turned into Katie's bedroom and bath. This made it Katie's room, with Katie's bed, Katie's desk, Katie's sofa, Katie's dresser, Katie's TV. Katie moved into this room because she had to have her own bath. With her winning that argument, the only option was the bonus room with her own outside door. I never liked this room, Katie's room. It's so far removed from the main part of the house. I never knew if she was home except if her car was parked in the driveway. This was a perfect fit for her.

Daddy easily picks me up from the wheelchair and places me on the vast, empty hospital bed. Folding up the wheelchair, his moves are quick, and everybody suddenly leaves. Now who can hear me since I'm the only one who will be living way back here?

Peggy Kohlmeyer

Looking around the room, Katie's bed and desk are gone. Instead, there is a huge, white hospital bed, but thankfully, they did leave her TV. Oddly, her short sofa or love seat is still here. With the room destitute of people except for me, a feeling of isolation overwhelms me as the hospital bed envelopes me. I'm feeling so lost and alone, looking at all the hollow space where my body is resting on the bed. A senselessness starts to creep in again as I look down, and all I see is white on white. My alabaster white skin on the white hospital bed. A quick feeling of emptiness encircles me that as always, I'm simply blending in. Why doesn't this make sense? Understanding white sheets, I'm just not sure why both of my legs are so white. Seeing them, they don't look like my legs, but wiggling my toes, they have to be mine. My mind is so empty. I wish I knew what's going on…

Placing my hand on my right leg, I notice the texture is hard and tough. Again, I wiggle my toes. This is a silly, childish reassurance that yes, those toes are mine. Looking at my left leg, I see my skin at the top and then a hard, white, rough part that is covering below my knee. Wiggling my toes on my left foot, I make the same successful association that they, too, belong to me. But if those are my toes and I can wiggle them, what's the white on my legs covering each one up? To add to it all, why did Daddy have to lift me up? Why didn't I simply stand? Making a bend in my left leg, I feel something scratchy on the top side of my foot.

As Katie's coming into her old bedroom, I look to her, asking her, "Why can't I see my legs?"

Grinning with a wry smile, she replies, "You're crazy. You can. You just have a cast on each one of them."

Peggy Kohlmeyer

Casts? I have two casts on? Why do I have a cast on each of my legs? Accepting this, I ask her, "Katie, what's scratching my left foot back and forth?"

Bending down to look at the cast and pulling some cotton out, Katie is trying to solve the reason for my itch, but it's still there. "I don't know, just ignore it and it will go away," leaving me puzzled as she goes back out the bedroom door.

Two casts. I have two casts. One on each leg. My mind again fades.

"I have to pee," I say to the next person who walks into the room.

"Let me get you the bedpan," is their quick response. A bedpan? Only people who are in the hospital use a bedpan. Pulling myself up, I realize that I can't even lift my body. Something so simple, yet I can't even pull myself up to sit up straight in the bed.

Quickly recapping my day, I remember that I've only observed what others are doing. Thinking of everything that's happened, I realize that I haven't done anything for myself. Katie had to scratch my foot, I had to be fed, and someone else had to hold the water when I wanted to drink. What's happened to me?

Time passing from minutes to hours and into even a day, people visit this back room checking on me. With each visit, they ask, "Are you OK? Do you want anything?" I'm embarrassed that I can't even answer them without getting upset. Look at me! I want to shout. I'm not OK, I don't know what's wrong with me! Even more, how did I get this way? What did I do to deserve this?

Seeing the bathroom and a connection of knowing where I have to go, I don't give myself any applause for something so simple that I have to pee.

Peggy Kohlmeyer

Starting to cramp with anguish from holding it so long, I'm frustrated and mad that I don't know how to get there, to get to the bathroom, to simply pee. Oh, my bladder hurts so badly and then…I'm too late for even using the bedpan, with a sudden liquid warmth between my legs. Embarrassing myself. I've wet my bed. How did I do that? I mean, I couldn't even hold it. It's my own bladder, and yet I couldn't even control it. I had to go, and I went, and someone is quickly here to clean up my own mess up.

My mind starts to fade, but this time it's from my personal shame.

I've got to begin with a list of things for me to do, to accomplish for my inner feeling of success. I'll start small with the things that people take for granted. The things that I should do but just can't. The goal for today is to do anything for myself like hold my own drink, hold my own fork, hold a pencil to write, or an overall goal of making it to the bathroom by myself. Simple things first, but those that are most important. I'll begin with feeding myself.

Looking at the fork on the bed tray in front of me, I know it is something that I have to grasp. My eyes are making the connection with the fork, my fingers know to grab the fork. Reaching it and touching it, the metal handle grants me that sudden cool chill of success. My sudden elation quickly bursts with disappointment since I can't even lift the fork in my right hand. I can't even hold my right hand up. A tear from my eye slides down my cheek. Exasperation and personal frustration are now overwhelming me. What's wrong with me that my own muscles won't allow me to lift up a stupid fork? This is another question that I can't even answer, that I've categorized as the unknown.

Peggy Kohlmeyer

Just as quickly as my anger sets in, I am crying over something as simple as this. A fork, a fork, lifting up a stupid fork! I have to refocus to accomplish my goal. I have to have a new strategy to try.

A quick thought enters my mind: my left hand; let's see what it can do. Going through the same steps, I see the fork, I know the fork, and I touch it. The same chill from the metal handle rewards me for the identical feeling that was originally a thrill. Now my big test is to actually pick it up, to actually lift up the fork. Oh, my gosh, what thought do I have think to command lifting the fork up from the tray? A deep breath, my heavy sigh and then only thinking *lift*.

There it goes! I've got it up, and I've got it down. I'm lifting this fork back and forth. Wow! I've made my goal for the moment, for the day.

OK, so I went from being a right-hander to a left-hander to feed myself. Ambidextrous now, well, maybe I can brag about that. Now using my left hand and putting the food in my mouth, my bite doesn't seem quite right. I can't bite. Oh, my gosh, I can't chew. I'm only gumming my food as if I don't have any teeth.

Dropping the fork with this harsh realization and starting to cry, I realize even more, something really bad has happened to me. Reflecting back to everything I know, I glance down to see that I'm in a hospital bed at home. Seeing it when I came into Katie's old bedroom, I didn't know that it was for me. The only role I've had is one of dazed and confused of everything. I've lost my identity, not actively participating. How many days? What's up with me? I'm not even able to make the connection to reality. What's wrong with me? Two casts, my right hand doesn't work, I can't lift a fork to feed

myself, and now I find out that I can't even chew

my own food. Who do I ask? Who will tell me what

else is wrong with my body? How much will I have

to learn on my own?

With these thoughts stirring around in my mind,

there is no one around to talk to or even ask. Almost in

a time warp as I fade in and out, I wonder how many

days it has been. Has someone been here, and I didn't

even remember? Asking myself these questions, I

already know the answers. Yes, people have been here

to see me and to take care of me, but except for my

body, mentally I haven't been here with them.

"Katie, what is wrong with me? Why

can't I get up? Why can't I do anything but lie in

this hospital bed? I'm so dependent, I can't even

get up to go and pee."

"What? You mean you don't know what has been going on?" Katie somberly states, "You were in an accident."

An accident. I was in an accident. Katie's simple statement explains a lot. An accident that has left me incapacitated of many of my simple bodily functions. Something happened that was so severe that it placed me in the hospital. An accident that has robbed me of my goals and identity. What did I do? How did I make it happen? These are the questions that I have to answer myself.

"I think I had it worse, though," Katie chirps, breaking up my moment of self-remorse. "I was the one that had to go to Saint Mary's Hospital and identify you." Katie's comment seems at first to rescue me of my sudden guilt. The guilt of what I have done and the consequences to everyone else around me.

Peggy Kohlmeyer

"You looked totally gross. Your chin wasn't even on your face."

Dropping my mouth open in disbelief and questioning the statement that she's just made, I'm trying to comprehend this picture. My chin wasn't even on my face? Katie's statement quickly has me wondering wherever else my chin could've been. Maybe realizing my confusion, Katie eloquently replies, "Freddie Kruger paid you a visit, and it wasn't even Friday the thirteenth."

Wow! What warm words to hear from one who supposedly loves you. I didn't look gross, but I looked totally gross. My chin wasn't even on my face. If Katie is saying that, then what does my face, my chin, my body look like now? How really gross am I? How really ugly am I now?

I was in an accident? Trying so hard to put some pieces of nothing together but understanding that's the reason we left Saint Francis Hospital. We weren't there to see Daddy. Daddy was there to bring me home. That's the reason that I was in a wheelchair. That's the reason for the lady in white. The nurse who wouldn't let me stand up. What kind of accident would explain my legs, my right arm, my mouth, and who knows what else?

Did I fall? Did I get hit crossing the street? What did I do that all this could've happened to me?

Regardless of how much time is passing or not, now I really have to make it to the bathroom. Having the double motivation to not only to pee, but to see how I look in the bathroom mirror. Katie says that Freddie Kruger paid me a visit. Remembering the ghastly, horrific previews of movies that I never went to see. I was too scared to see Freddy killing innocent people by slicing them up; with Katie's

comparison, how am I going to look? How sad is it

to depend on someone else to help me pee when I'm

twenty years old? Twenty years old? Is that my age?

Oh, my gosh, I just remembered my age. I feel it

now, I know what's going on, and my bladder is

telling me it's time for me to get up and go or call

someone again for the bedpan.

Goals, didn't somewhere, somehow, I have

goals? Aren't I now able to feed myself, even if it is

with my left hand instead of my right one? I've got

to start doing things for myself. I mean, *more* things

for myself. I've got to focus more. I have to face

reality. I've got to get rid of these people trying to

help me all the time. I've got to stop fading in and

out of reality.

Pee? Yes, now a true connection that I can

always depend. When my bladder starts to hurt,

that's the prompt that I've relearned. It simply means I've got to go and pee. For the bigger step or my next goal; my biggest goal yet is to make it to the bathroom on my own.

This is going to take a plan of reasonable moves. With time and strategy, I'll have to start with putting my feet on the floor, while holding on to the hospital bed rail. I can guide myself to the end of the bed, grab the wall, inching myself down to the bathroom door, and then touch the bathroom sink, followed by the toilet. Visualizing my plan is the easiest part, but now, let's just see how this all goes. Will my body even follow?

Touching the metal bed rail, I'm going to have hold this for a lot of stability until I make it standing up. I've got to get my left foot on the ground. Maybe if I just swing it over to the side of the bed like this, *swoosh*. Hey, it's done.

Peggy Kohlmeyer

With a short cast only halfway up my leg, I'm actually able to bend my left knee, placing my foot on the floor. Next is my right leg. With the cast all the way up to my hip, this is going to take some major work. I've got to swing my right leg over, but since it doesn't bend, I've got to pop my body up at the same time to stand. I'm sweating just trying to get out of bed. Gosh, who would have thought that getting out of bed could be such work.

OK, here it goes...*Swoosh, pop.* Wow, I made it! I'm standing, but I've got to remember to breathe. *Huff, huff* is all that I can hear from myself as I start to pant, holding on to my moment of glory. Holding the bed rail, gosh, this is a feeling of inner success. How many months has it been since I've even been able to stand?

Forget the glory, now I've got to continue to make my goal. Step, slide my hand, step, slide my hand. Hey, this is working. I'm taking a side step and sliding my hand down the side of the bed. One more step, one more slide of my hand. I'm able to steady myself as I move toward the bathroom. Now I'm at the end of the bed. Deep breath, reaching out and finally touching the wall. Yes, it's farther than I thought.

Breathe! I've got to remember to breathe. Reach for the wall!

Another success I've made. With a cast on each leg, it's neat how I can use them to sway a little bit back and forth. Let's try it again. Step first, then placing my hand, step again, move my hand again. OK, my plan is great; at least I've reached the bathroom door. I need a break; this is just so hard.

Looking back over the path to the bathroom that I just took, I'm leaning on my right leg, since it is stiff and straight, with the cast almost up to my crotch. My left leg, with the cast only up to my knee, allows me to navigate. Hey, my legs are like the paddles in a boat. One paddle to steer and the other for motion. Now I only need to bend at my waist to touch the bathroom sink. Step, move my hand, and I'm there.

Next the toilet: step, slide my hand for the last reach…and yes, I make it, I'm at the toilet. Oh, my gosh, I've made it to the bathroom without anyone here to help me! Success! Success!

But now how am I going to sit? I can't even bend my right knee to sit down. How is my whole body going to get there, to lower myself to the toilet? Why do they make bathroom toilets so low to the ground? Wait, a new plan. If I reverse my action of getting out of bed, instead of raising myself up, now I will only have to lower myself down. I've only got to hold on to the bathroom wall instead of the bed rail and bend my left leg first, and then plop down onto the toilet seat. Sure, that's what I can do.

Urination is the responsibility I missed for months, depending on a catheter. I never thought it was something that I took for granted. Oh, my gosh, I've got to pee! "*Help*!"

Days of isolation in Katie's back bedroom continue to pass. "Peggy, the bed and the wall get you to the bathroom, but it's time you started getting out more. Getting out more like to the rest of the house," Daddy says to me with a grin and an encouraging voice, as he is bent at the waist, leaning over a huge metal contraption.

Asking him with puzzlement, "What's this?"

"A walker."

"A walker? How does it work?"

"You just put your hands on the metal bars to support you. Instead of using the wall, you'll use this." Daddy demonstrates for me to copy him, "First you take a step, then you lift the walker up. Next, you move it out in front of you and place it back down.
There, you see, you've got a step."

"Oh, OK." Looking at it, I'm already having a fear that it's not going to work. Giving a sigh, I put my feet on the floor. This part of me getting out of bed I pretty much like. It's neat to have my body pop up with my right leg in a full-length cast and surprise people when they watch me.

Standing up, reaching over to the walker, I'm leaning on it. I take a step, but I can't move it. I can't move the walker. I can take another step, and I can lean on it, but I can't lift the metal contraption up. If I still can't support a fork or spoon in my right hand to feed myself, how am I supposed to lift the metal frame of a walker? I feel like I am adding insult to my injury. My mind isn't making the connection to rest on the metal frame while I'm supposed to try and lift it up. Even worse, I don't have any upper body strength to lift it. This is almost like a balancing act, too. I see that I am supposed to balance or stand on my own two feet, which I can't do. My legs aren't stable or strong enough to hold me upright. If I simply stand up, I can rest on the walker, but I can't move the walker in front of me like Daddy did. Feeling stranded in my own room, I cannot move. With exasperation, my body is just stuck resting on it. What a failure I am! I can't even lift a metal walker to help myself.

Peggy Kohlmeyer

"Peg, try these," Daddy says the next time he comes into the room.

"What are those?"

"Crutches."

"Crutches? How do those work?"

"You put them under your arms to stabilize you as you stand. Here, you try."

"OK, I've got it. They go up under my armpits."

"That's right, now place them in front of you when you want to take a step."

"In front of me? If I place them in front of me, then what am I going to balance on?"

"Here, let me show you. You're standing here, like this, with the pads under your armpits. You put one foot out and have the other one follow, and just repeat to move along."

"Let me try." This looks easier than the previous walker. I pop myself out of bed again to try and wrestle with another walking apparatus. With the padded rests under my armpits, the first step is easy enough. Placing the posts in front of me, I have that part down.

Now one foot, let's make it the right, followed by the left. Not too bad, but there is something wrong here.

"Daddy, if I'm moving my legs, why does my side hurt?"

"Your side hurts? Peg, what do you mean?"

"Right here, under my arm."

"Oh, Peg, I forgot all about that. That's the incision where the tube was placed to inflate your lung."

"What do you mean?"

Peggy Kohlmeyer

"Your right rib was fractured. It punctured your lung, collapsing it, and a tube was inserted to basically inflate it.

"Oh, I didn't know that" is my comment, as if another secret has been let out.

Refocusing on my task at hand, using the crutches, I wonder how I can manipulate them to make them work. The crutches are fine. They hold me up, and I can balance on them. The problem comes every time I take a step or attempt to, with the padding on the armrest that rubs me raw.

"Daddy look, the scab is starting to bleed."

"Peg, we'll give these up, too. You tried. Let's just go back to the way you were getting around. You're doing a great job using the wall."

My lung was punctured? What else happened to me in that accident?

Ring...ring. Oh, my gosh, that's the phone. Daddy's phone! No one's here but me. Linda's gone to do errands and to the grocery store. Katie's over with John and his family. I've got to answer it. It could be the hospital. *Ring.* Easy enough, same sequence as before:left foot on the floor, deep breath, followed by my right foot, deep breath, and once again, *pop*, I'm up. Plan of action? I'll just use the same sequence as if I'm going to the bathroom, but this won't be a pit stop. I'll just continue to the hallway, the kitchen, and then the phone.

Ring, ring.

"Hold on, hold on! I'm coming."

Yay! Me making it to the bathroom is easy enough. Now new, uncharted territory. I'll only have to remember my trusted sequence of steps. I'll have to step and slide my hand, and step and slide my hand. Easy enough repetition for me to

follow. Leaning on the bonus room door frame,

"Hello, hallway," stepping into the doorway that

leads from the bonus room to the hall thinking,

wow, I forgot how long this was.

Never mind, just concentrate. "Step, slide my

hand, step, slide my hand," with me saying it out

loud, it seems that I'm moving just a bit faster, with

almost a steady rhythm going down the hall.

"Wow," I say out loud, finally making it to the

kitchen. Looking back, I express my appreciation

with a smile for the carpet, instead of a tiled floor

since I didn't have a chance to slip and fall.

Ring, ring.

"I know you're ringing, phone. I'm coming,

have patience." Now that I'm in the doorway of the

kitchen, looking around, there's no wall for me to

hold on to. There's only the kitchen counter all the

way over there. Can I reach it? Will I make it? Thinking this out, I'll keep my left hand on the door frame and my left foot by the door. This will keep me stable. Saying it out loud to myself for needed assurance, "With my right leg in the full cast, place it a step toward the kitchen counter." This is it. Deep breath. Swing myself over, just rocking on my right cast, reach, reach, reach, touching the counter. Yay!

Ring.

No fear. Now I'll just step and slide my hand around on the edge of the counter. I'm down to the turn and one more step.

"Hello."

"Peg, this is your dad. How did you answer the phone?"

"Oh, Daddy, I thought it was important. Your phone was ringing, and you weren't here. I thought it could be the emergency room or the hospital or your office."

"Oh, Peg, it is important. I was calling to see how you are doing."

The haze of my days continues, but clarity in my mind is returning in larger amounts, along with longer empty spells. I get the explanation the next day that takes me by storm. "Peggy, you've got a telephone call in the kitchen. Can you get it?" Linda asks me, walking into the bonus room.

"Sure, just give me a minute." Or two, or three, or twenty. I mean, seriously, they'll have to wait. Finally, with me reaching the kitchen phone, "Yes, this is Peggy."

"Hi, I'm calling from the Athens *Banner Herald*, and I'm doing a follow-up story to the drunk driver who hit you. What do you think of the suicide that resulted when the judge gave him his sentence?"

A car accident? A drunk driver? What is this person saying? What's going on here? Why is he calling, and what is he asking me? OK, yes, I was in an accident, but a car accident, hit by a drunk driver? No, not me. That could never happen to me.

"Miss Pike, is there anything that you would like to say?"

"I'm not sure; I don't know what to say."

"Well, how did you feel when Mr. Ed Hayes came to visit you at Saint Mary's?"

"Ed Hayes? Who is Ed Hayes? No, you're wrong. It seems that you have called the wrong person, I was at Saint Francis in Columbus, Georgia, not Saint Mary's Hospital in Athens."

"Yes ma'am, that's where you were transferred after your accident, but you started off at Saint Mary's when you were in Athens."

Peggy Kohlmeyer

"Why would I have been at Saint Mary's in Athens? My dad works at Saint Francis in Columbus."

"Oh, I see, Miss Pike. We understand; we'll give you a call later. Thank you."

A car accident? I was in a car accident in Athens, Georgia? That's what happened to me? Then how did I get to Columbus, Georgia?

"Daddy, Katie, what is this person talking about that I was in a car accident? How could I be in a car accident?"

"What Peg? You didn't know?" Dad says, almost with embarrassment. "We took it for granted that you knew what happened. Katie, go get Peg the scrapbook that you've made for her. That's the best way for her to see everything."

"What?" is all I ask myself. I was in a car accident? Why didn't they tell me? What did they think I was thinking? Even more, they didn't know that I wasn't thinking. Not thinking at all for myself.

"Gosh, Katie, this scrapbook is so heavy, so fat. This is all about me? You did this for me?"

"I wasn't sure what to do with all the flowers and cards that you got. There were so many, and they were so pretty, but you would never see them. Instead, I collected the cards that were on them, and I just started gluing them in these two scrapbooks."

"Wow, this is just so big."

"Let's start here. Here's the first article that appeared in the newspaper after you were hit, "A Night of Horror," from the Athens *Observer*. Talk about hot off the press. This is the Friday after your accident on Monday."

"That picture is my tenth-grade picture from high school. How'd they get that?"

"I don't know. I just collected the stuff, I didn't ask about it."

"It says June seventeenth. That's the day that it happened?"

"Yes, a Monday night. After the first day of your summer classes at Georgia."

"You mean I was going to school during the summer?"

"You know, you were just finishing up, then after your internship in the fall you would graduate."

"Katie what's today's date?"

"September, September tenth, why?"

It's already September, and I just got out of the hospital. That means June, July, August, and the first part of September…boy, how much time have I lost? How much have I missed?

"Katie, this article states that you talked to the reporter. You didn't tell me that."

"You didn't ask. I didn't know what you knew. Now it seems that you don't know very much."

"This article says that my teeth were knocked out. Meaning that is the reason that I've got this big gap?" pointing to my mouth.

"Come on, Peg, haven't you noticed that you haven't been able to chew or eat?"

"Yeah, but since I don't remember anything from before, how I would know anything is different, especially about not having my front teeth?"

"Then I take it you can't remember anything that happened back then? You mean nothing?"

A haze, that's what I've been going though, almost a complete haze, a detachment from reality.

"Katie, don't do this to me. I can't tell you what I *can* remember and *can't* remember because I just don't know. I mean, I don't know what I'm even supposed to know," in frustrated puzzlement.

"Well it was June, and you were doing your last semester at Georgia. The town was pretty empty except for the students staying for the summer. I got this phone call from Daddy saying that you've been in an accident. When we got to Saint Mary's the emergency room nurse said that you were very fortunate. An EMT on duty knew you, matching your picture on your driver's license, and the doctors were able to go ahead and started working on you.

"Any idea who it was who saw me, who identified me? Did I know them?"

"Oh yes, remember Ray from Clarke Central? You're lucky he was the EMT on duty. He knew you. He identified you. When he identified your body, everything moved so much faster. The doctors would have waited on us to come and see you, to make sure it was you."

"Waited? Waited for what?"

"Waited to work on you. I mean, to the extent that they did. Your face, your foot, your legs, and then your breathing."

"I could have been worse off than I am now?"

"Worse off than what? You were pretty bad when we made it to the hospital and confirmed that you were you, that you were my sister. I had to look at you to say I knew you, but then after I saw you, it's like I regretted it," Katie shares as her hand gently rests on my shoulder. Covering her fear by not looking at me in the face, looking down at the hospital bed, she continues, "Keep reading the article."

Peggy Kohlmeyer

As I surprise myself, reading is something that I am able to do. "Her leg was broken in two places, her feet so badly mangled that they had to be wired together. Her collarbone was broken, and she's in a coma." A coma, a coma, I was in a coma?

"Katie, is this be the reason I can't remember anything?" Recovering from a coma is the reason for my haze. My mind starts clicking adding the injuries that I know about. My collarbone was broken. That's why I can't use my right arm. Which is why I can't use my right hand. I can't walk since I've got a cast on each leg. And I can't use crutches due to a scab from a tube in my side to help my lung.

"Mom pretty much lost it when you didn't pick her up at the airport."

"I was supposed to pick Mom up at the airport?" Hmm, Mom at the airport, why? Picturing

Mom, I just don't know the connection between her and the airport. Airport? Questioning whatever is an airport anyway?

Continuing, Katie fills me in, "She was coming back from Africa again this summer, and you were supposed to pick her up." Mom? Our mom living in Africa? What is Katie talking about? I mean, Mom and Daddy have always been divorced, and Mom would never be in Columbus with Daddy, but I don't understand where Mom is now, except that I'm in Columbus, and this is Daddy's town, where Mom has never been welcomed.

Now my mind is screwing up, but I'm still desperately trying to focus. I can't fade out. This is the explanation I need. Once more, turning the scrapbook pages with more cards expressing support. I see cards of sympathy. Looking through this scrapbook, all I see is page after page after page of "A speedy recovery," "Thinking of you," "Get well soon," enclosure cards from the flowers sent to me that Katie's saved. With the turning of each page, I'm almost holding my breath, hoping for some definitive answer to what happened to me. It's like I am searching for the needed details, trying to solve my own mystery. Looking closely, reading each card, some are from family, some from friends, but then those from businesses and people I don't even know.

Finally nearing the end and feeling disillusioned for not receiving a hint or an answer, with exasperation, I'm ready to close the book, turning to the last page. There are not any more cards. Instead articles, newspaper articles about my accident. Yes, my time and due diligence have paid off. This is the section that has been waiting for me.

These articles are neatly arranged as if in a particular order, as a sequence of events.

The first article strikes me, popping out at me as an invitation for me to read its bold title, "Family of DUI victim speaks out on grief, tragedy of accident." Glancing over the article, I realize that I'm reading, once again actually reading it. The information is also making sense to me. I quickly thank myself for not missing that aspect of my brain. Questioning myself as to how long it's been since I've used my brain to read. I gleefully recognize its importance to place on my daily to-do list. Momentarily hesitating, pondering this thought and new task, I move on, devouring and reading what the article says.

"She started her last semester," and "She got into her Mazda" places the context of the article with the sense of someone else, because with everything that I've read, it's another person that they are writing about. Finding some more newspaper articles that are pasted and equally arranged, my curiosity continues about this girl, this individual, having to remind myself that I'm really searching for information about me.

My eyes glancing to the left side of the page and getting hit as if with a blow to my head, I read the titles: "Father Wins Battle Over Hurt Daughter," "Father Wins Custody of Injured Coed," and "UGA Student Is Being Moved to Hospital Near Her Home." Aghast with this information, I begin to examine each article as if I'm a spy, collecting information on myself.

...went to probate court Monday seeking temporary emergency guardianship of her twenty-year-old daughter...well enough to travel...to give her time to rest, and every day she gets better...the

judge dismissed mother's request for temporary

guardianship but requested that she not be moved.

"Katie, where's Mom now?"

"She had to go back to work. She went back to Africa."

When I was in sixth grade and class got boring, I could just sit and stare. Nope, I wasn't staring at anyone or anything in particular, I was just gazing into space. For me, I was on stalled time. People around me could easily tell, since I would get my dazed look, with both of my eyes getting a little larger not making connection to anyone or anything. Mentally, I hadn't gone anywhere in particular, only removing myself from what was going on around me. It wasn't meant as an insult to others; instead, this was my answer and alternative to reality. I felt mentally that I had better places to visit or memories to relive, and sometimes I simply got bored.

Peggy Kohlmeyer

Attempting to re-connect from this easy mental escape left me totally clueless of those immediate events that had happened around me.

Making note of this, Katie coined this time for me as my "la-la land." It really didn't bother me that she used this term toward me. It made me feel that at least she was paying attention to me, and her term actually did fit. Now, though, it's like I am totally clueless as to what is going on or what is happening in my life. Rather than escaping for a moment to la-la land, I am constantly fighting with myself to reconnect or focus to stay in touch. Heck, I just had to learn to pee on my own again.

My fading in and out happens so much now that I can't even keep track of my days. The months of June, July, August, and the first part of September have been completely lost, with no mental connections to where I have been, what has happened to me, and the people around me who have even showed they cared. Even more, the question that I'm asking myself is what am I doing with my life now?

With me making it to the great room or family room in Daddy's house, Katie's doing what I realize I can still do: reading. I ask her with a little bit of envy, "What are you reading?"

"Not a favorite, but what I have to read for school. Let me get the books that you had at Georgia."

School? That's right. I was at Georgia when this happened. That means that I had to attend classes, and I had classwork to do. That means that I also had to read.

Opening the book at the top of the stack, *The Iliad* by Homer, turning to the first page, and trying to read the first paragraph: *Sing O goddess, the anger of Achilles son of Peleus, that brought countless ills upon the Achaeans. Many a brave soul did it send hurrying down to Hades, and many a her did it yield a prey to dogs and vultures...*Not realizing it, I let out a groan.

"What? What's wrong? Peg, what is it?"

"Oh, sorry. I think I picked the wrong one."

"*The Iliad*? You picked up *The Iliad to read*? Peg, you shouldn't even have to ask. That's one of your books for your Greek literature class."

Looking through the others in the stack, Katie pulls out one that looks really old but causes me to grin.

"Here, try this one." She hands it to me and says, "*The Book of Running.*"

Running? Looking down at my two casts while covering my inside laugh; why did I have a book of running? "What's up with this? I mean, why do I have it?" Pausing for Katie to think.

"You had some idea that you were going to do that race in Atlanta, the Peachtree Road Race."

Not quite sure what to make of it, but a book that I will definitely read and maybe, just maybe, it will become my longtime, ultimate goal.

My first venture out of the house is in the back seat of the family van which is almost twofold in its purpose. First of all, Daddy is so generous for this ride because this is time for him away from his work and patients. Also, I see it as time meant for just us. In the van with no distractions for either of us, I'm trying to get the courage to ask him about the question Katie had about me not having my period.

Daddy's a doctor, so in the medical sense he knows about that, and yet I haven't had the bravery even to ask him or approach the subject. How does any girl talk to her dad about something like this?

For Daddy, our endeavor out lets him think that he is helping me overcome some type of fear that I have of being on the road. Some people have claimed that my body is the evidence of the devastation of getting hit head on by a drunk driver, but it wasn't me. Reading the newspaper articles in the scrapbook that Katie made, it wasn't me who had that accident. Sure it's Peggy, and that's who I am, and my body was there, but mentally I wasn't.

Pretty much I'm thankful that I went into a coma, right on impact as one of the articles states. Mentally I'm not making any connection since I have no reflection to associate or comprehend. It's

only my body that was going to the University of
Georgia to complete the last semester of classes,
but not me. I am here, and right now I don't have a
fear of the road, especially when Daddy drives.
Why doesn't anyone understand that?

"Peg, you're comfortable back there?"

"Of course, and it's great to see the
outside again. I forgot how great it is to simply
breath fresh air."

"I forgot about the air. You have been
inside for a while."

"Well, yeah Dad, I have a question or
even a concern."

"Yes, Peg?"

"Katie mentioned something to me that
I'm not sure about, and I really don't know how
to ask you."

"Well, you already have. You started with a question about asking it, so just ask."

"Daddy, why haven't I had my period? I mean, I had it before, right? So why aren't I having it now?"

"Peg, that's what you're so concerned about? Look at what you have been through. Look at the size of your body. Your body has more important things to take care of than your monthly menstrual cycle."

"Oh."

"Let's just give it a little more time. When your body is back in check, you'll see it pick back up. Just think of this as a break from dealing with that."

"Look at the traffic. What's up?"

The fast food hamburger chain Krystal is the final destination for our first road trip. As my reward for leaving the house, Daddy simply states, "Peg, get anything that you want."

This is easily accomplished with my order, "Just a small chocolate milkshake." Understanding that the hospital IVs were my sole form of nourishment for three months, the straw of a chocolate shake is fitting perfectly into the gaping front of my toothless mouth. While attempting my initial slurp of the shake through the straw, I'm reminded how great it is to have something cool and refreshing hit some of my taste buds. Eroding my simple pleasure and slowly encompassing all my thought processes, the missing idea that eventually registers into my mind as I savor the chocolate taste going down: "Oh, this is going to make me fat." Needless to say, my ritual of caloric guilt is reborn. As soon as we get back home, two casts and all, I'm having to find the bathroom scale. *Look at the size*

of your body are the words I'm remembering Daddy
saying. Weighing in, holding on to the bathroom
wall for that still needed stability, the scale reads 87
pounds.

"What, 87 pounds? Who messed with my
scale?" Stepping off, thinking it's a lie, making sure
the red line goes back to 0, and it does. Stepping
back on again. I get the same number for my weight,
87 pounds. Totally confused, I repeat this process
one more time. Again, I weigh 87 pounds.
Murmuring to myself, "What's wrong with this
scale? I don't understand, how can I only weigh 87
pounds? I mean, I'm 133, and I've got two casts on.
This doesn't make any sense." Wow, for all the
things for me to remember, 133 pounds.
Recognizing it as the weight that I've always fought,
saying it out loud makes me have a quick, rewarding
chill. I can't believe I'm remembering that,

especially now feeling there is no way this can be right, and looking down again, all I see is 87.

Previously, every day I had a routine. After a morning pee and not eating breakfast, I'd weigh myself, since I'd be at my lowest weight for the day. If I was at 130, it made a great day. Meaning for a few days I could splurge on tastes I felt that I'd earned: ice cream, pizza, or even a chocolate chip cookie. Careless of counting calories, I savored these delicacies until that morning weight again shouted 132, 133, or even the dreaded 135. Alas, the same routine would ensue, having to face the next few days with the dread of only watching others eat these treats, and me attempting to slim back down.

Looking down at my body now, it's registering that something really did happen to me since numbers never lie. 87 pounds? That's just sick.

Peggy Kohlmeyer

"This isn't real. 87 pounds is a weight that I've never, ever weighed, not even in my biggest fantasy." Just as quickly, making this statement out loud, I dismiss it to that other person, not me. Since I'm five feet, ten inches, my desired weight is always 125. Having been there once, it put me on the slim side, not having to argue with my clothes to fit. Right now? This isn't me. I could never get as low as this.

Going out for another daily ride, I'm expecting more great, tasteful rewards. I mean, the first was the trip to Krystal Hamburgers; the second trip is to my dad's favorite restaurant, Los Amigos. You're guessing right if you say Mexican, since it's easy to assume by its name. My taste buds are revitalized again due to the spicy kick of the signature hot sauce. Spicy or sweet, both of my favorite tastes are now reclaimed.

Sitting in Los Amigos, I hesitate to eat anything at first. Everything I've eaten so far has been diluted like baby food. With that aside, I'm more curious at what's on the table, peering at the basket of tortilla chips Maria delivers. Following everyone else, I also pick up a chip. I hesitate and examine it closely as to how and where to place it in my mouth. Hmm, I'm thinking. I can't chew with my front teeth since they're not there. But I have to have an alternative for this experience.

"Ugh" expresses my exasperation, gently placing the broken parcel of a chip on my tongue. Instantly, the taste of the picante sauce kicks in! My taste buds are reawakened again. Wow, what a tasty reward. The chip is still crisp. I let it sit to soften with my salvia. Rolling it around in my mouth, I find some sort of my teeth on the left back side of my mouth seem to be intact. Slowly and thoughtfully, I chew so as not to poke and prod it into my gums. The basket is finished with the help of everyone else. My entree? A Burrito, with Daddy's guidance of what is easier for me to eat. It can't be much of a problem with the soft shell. Every time I bite down, I have to place my teeth gently into my gums. This must be the way the elderly eat without their dentures, but once again I'm rediscovering the joyful tastes of food.

Rather than for lunch or dinner, the third ride is happening in the morning. This timing is raising my suspicions about our destination, but since Daddy's the sole driver, why should I worry? Pulling into the Saint Francis Hospital, thinking this is his normal routine of dropping by and checking in on his patients as the real reason we left home so early. Instead, Daddy is parking the van and opening up my door. Seeing a wheelchair on the curb, my inner alarm starts. This trip is for me. Tears find a way to slowly slide down my face. Looking at Daddy with my mournful expression of "Why?"

"Peg, we have to get the metal studs out of your gums."

Metal studs in my gums? I question myself and the reason for this trip, while my tongue glides slowly over the actual metal post still anchored above my teeth in my gums. "After your jawbone fractured, pegs or studs were placed to wire your mouth shut. Your jaw had to get realigned."

Oh, my gosh, that's what those metal things are? Running my tongue over the area above my teeth, along my gum line, I'm feeling each individual stud. Hmm, remembering my initial wonderment of what those things were. Yes, of course I knew they were there, I mean, since

they're in my mouth, but I had no idea that's what
they were.

"It's simple outpatient surgery with an
anesthesiologist putting you to sleep, so you won't
feel a thing," Daddy's telling me as my mind
wants to panic. No, I'm not scared of the surgery,
and I'm not scared of being put to sleep, but I hate
going back to a place where I've already lost so
much time.

Lying on the hospital cot. The guy with his
hair covered and dressed in blue medical scrubs is
holding a needle, looking at the veins in my arm.
With him looking and looking, I'm not sure where
that long needle is going, but his apprehension is
killing me. Again, a single tear slides down my
face: fear.

"I'm sorry miss, I just can't find a vein."

Find a vein? That's what he's looking for? He's implying that needle is going to go into my arm? His answer gives me the reality that now I'm going to be put to sleep, and I am scared.

"It looks like that they've all been used, and I can't find a strong one."

A strong one, he's saying, and suddenly I act with impertinence. "Where do you think I've been?" Asking myself, turning my head in disgust as Daddy approaches to check the progress.

"Peg, make a fist with your left hand, let it go, make a fist again, and hold it."

Ouch! Daddy to the rescue, I guess. He found my vein, but boy does that hurt. Afterward, calling myself peg-free, I'm in recovery and back home by 10:00 a.m. Realizing, though, that I have to find me, myself, and start my life again. I've also got to find an alternative way to spend my mornings.

Peggy Kohlmeyer

My days are coming and going, and I'm getting up more and getting around. My list of things to do each day is getting quite long. Some things I don't even write on the list anymore because it's understood that I have to do them. Like going to the bathroom. Heck, who ever had to have that listed to complete? OK, me. Only so I could check it off with my earned success, but now since it's a given, I don't. Now I only write the important or new tasks down. Also, I'm relearning things every day. Simple things that I took for granted. Like if I'm thirsty, it means that I need some water.

Daddy has a cool, front-water-dispensing refrigerator, which means that I never have to worry about getting the ice. I only have to worry about getting to the kitchen. This event begins with me leaving my bedroom and calling for some help, since the hallway is dark. Katie simply shouts, "If you can't see, just turn on the light."

Turn on the light? Great idea, but how?

Getting out of her seat, since she's watching TV, Katie comes into the hallway and simply flips up a switch.

"Oh, I didn't know" is all I can say, feeling utterly clueless and embarrassed. "*Humph*," I let out in exasperation. Registering this event as something else I've relearned: if it is dark, simply turn on the light. This making it easier to get my water whenever I want.

With the count of my road trips at two, plus one that doesn't count since it was back to the hospital, I'm not sure what to expect when we make another road trip. My fourth trip out turns out to be the same as trip number three, or another trip back to the hospital. This time it's for

my leg. Yes, the right one, which later I call the
wrong one since this is the reason for my trip.

Daddy is trying to express some cheer as he
explains the need for my visit. He breaks it down
with as little medical jargon as possible. "Peg, your
leg has settled. Your compound fracture has not
mended where it needed to."

OK, I've got that, but I'm thinking about
what he has said and trying to decipher the real
message he's trying to send me.

"An X-ray shows that your right leg is one
or two inches shorter than its original length…and
shorter in comparison to your left leg."

Shorter? That doesn't make sense. How can
one of my legs get shorter than the other? I'm
totally puzzled now, trying to figure this out.

"The plan involves taking part of your hip,
your right hip, and placing it to fill in the space

where your leg has settled. With this done, you'll have both legs equal in length again."

OK, I understand this. Looking up at Daddy, a slight grin crosses my face, expressing my simple appreciation for him being who he is, and then:

"Your appointment this morning is to rebreak your right leg."

Hearing what Dad is actually saying, I now realize this is bad news, totally bad news for me. Not only am I going back to the hospital again, but surgery, real surgery this time. That anesthesiologist, my veins, my hip, and then my leg.

"Good morning, welcome, Peggy," the nurse says as she's rolling me into the operating room. A first name greeting for me? No wonder, with all my time and visits, but it's kind of nice she's trying to put me at ease. Ease, though? I quickly remind myself, when I'm the one lying here on the hospital gurney.

Recognizing the same anesthesiologist as before, I'm making a fist, reminding him I know what to do. I guess it's never too late for anyone to learn, and this time working together, he'll have no problem trying to find my vein. That's it, I'm done, and the needle is in. Now only to worry about what I'm going to be like when I do recover.

Fortunately, my thinking and fears subside as I slide into a deep sleep.

"Peg." Waking up to Daddy's voice. "The X-ray proved more than what we thought."

Hmm? What? More than we thought? Is Daddy asking a question for me or making a statement to himself?

"You can say that your break is now the strongest part of your body. It's doubled in strength since it has the consistency of two bones."

Two bones? Now Daddy does have me puzzled but explains further.

"Having a forty-five-degree break, the top portion of your leg slid down."

Slide? How did my bone slide? It's a bone, and it had a break. Bones don't slide.

"Since its movement and your time in the hospital, the top portion now has a one-and-a-half-inch rest over the lower portion of your leg."

Did he just say one-and-a-half-inch difference? How? I don't understand. I still don't see how my bones can move.

"You didn't have the surgery. The difference is just too great to mend."

Whoa! Did he say no surgery? That is the best news that I could hear.

"You did get a new, water-resistant cast for when you want to swim again."

Swim? You want me to swim? If only I could walk to get out of here. Why would I ever swim?

"As I was saying, when you think about it," hearing Daddy's voice hitting a more jovial tone, "your right leg is now super strong."

But swim, when I want to swim? What did he mean by swim? This is something I'll have to check this out with Katie when I get home.

Katie's standing in front of the pantry, smacking her lips as I step and slide into the kitchen. I ask her, as I hear her crunching, "When we were at the hospital, why did Daddy say that about me swimming? I mean, where did he get that idea?" Having caught her munching on Doritos, I wonder why I haven't had any of these. "Hey, let me have one."

"Here, but you're not going to be able to chew it."

"Why not? What do you mean?"

"Peg, your teeth are all messed up. Remember, when we went to Los Amigos and you tried to eat those chips? You've only been eating soft stuff like soup, yogurt, and ice cream."

"Oh" is all I can say, since I hate it when Katie is right. Even when I'm shouting inside, "Yay!" knowing my next road trip is to see my dentist, Dr. Avant.

A warm feeling envelopes me as we pull into Dr. Avant's parking lot. Dr. Avant is my childhood dentist. Crossing my fingers this morning, again I'm banking on his dental magic. Growing up, no matter what dental tricks he performed, I always left with a

whiter, brighter, and better smile. This time my visit

is different. You can bet I'm counting on his dental

wizardly now.

Sitting in my wheelchair, getting pushed into his

front office, I'm thankful that his office is empty. After

the potato chip incident with Katie yesterday, I'm

embarrassed to smile. I can't smile since I don't have

the left front teeth or upper jawbone. If I do grin, I only

have a gaping, toothless hole.

"Peggy, good to see you" is the warm greeting

that, as always, I'm now receiving. "Let's just find out

what we have here." Dr. Avant casually stoops down

and lifts me to the examination chair.

"OK, Peggy, let's just open...and

close...good. Once again, open and close." Dr.

Avant's guiding me, checking out what bite I might

or might not have. Hearing his *hmm*s and seeing his head nod, I don't feel so bad.

The X-rays he's taking are a little hard since I can't actually bite down to hold the X-ray film. I realize the worst part is about to happen when he wants to make a mold of my mouth. Looking at the gray clay he is holding, my mind says, "Yuck." I'm still waiting for his miracle to happen and my teeth to reappear with the magic that Dr. Avant has. I'm realizing that it's only a wish, as Dr. Avant says, "Peg, we'll see you here next week."

Leaving Dr. Avant's office, which is close to Peachtree Mall, Daddy makes an easy swing into the mall parking lot. Noticing he's parking in a handicap parking space raises my curiosity; why? I mean, doctors do have their privileges, but to park here? Then I realize I'm the one who's handicapped. This parking place is for me. I'm glad that I kept my mouth shut on that one.

Going into Peachtree Mall, my anxiety starts to build. Dr. Avant's office is fine. He and his staff already know about me and my circumstances, but going into the mall? No one here knows my story. No one here is going to remember that I'm the one who was a weekly shopper. No one here is going to remember what I was like before and compare it to how I look now. Then again, if I don't remember all that much, what can I expect of them?

Calling it perfect timing or bad timing, entering through the women's wear side of Dillard's, I hear Daddy say, "Hi, Ms. Goins, what perfect timing," as a tall, thin lady steps off the down escalator.

"Hello, Dr. Peak, hello, Peggy, it's great to see that the two of you are getting out and about."

Who is this? Yet I'm too embarrassed to ask. As Daddy continues, "We were up the street at Peg's dentist and thought it would be a good idea to drop by and say hello."

"I'm certainly glad you did." She answers above my head with me sitting below in the wheelchair. As if I'm not even here, Ms. Goins shares, "We're holding her position for her whenever she is ready to get started."

Started? Whenever I am ready to get started? Started to do what? As they both nod at each other and Daddy rolls me farther into the store, "Daddy, who was that?"

"Oh, she is the human resource manager, Ms. Goins. You were to start your internship here next week."

Peggy Kohlmeyer

"Next week? How am I supposed to do that?"

"Peg, you heard her. Your spot has been saved. That's why I wanted to stop by. She needed to see you in person, to see how far you've come."

"Oh" is all I can say. Trying to get a handle on working. Working?

"Lucky girl, you surely impressed them with your interview.
You heard her. They're holding your spot."

My spot? Hold my spot? What was I going to do? Finish college, too? I'm supposed to start working and complete an internship? Now I'm hit with a sudden slap from the world of reality. I have to get my degree. That's my final step toward my independence and knowing I have to graduate from college. A fear sets in reminding myself I don't have a high school diploma.

Chapter 14
Tying Up Loose Ends

"Peggy, you've got some company."

Company? Who would want to come see me? Who do I know? It's summertime. And no one wants to spend time inside and with me.

"Peg, how you doin'? Kris sneakily says, peeking his head around the door.

Kris? Kris? Oh, my gosh, I know him, like, I really know him. But how? Who is this?

"Sorry it's taken me so long to get over here. I mean, after seeing you in Athens, it totally blew me away. Boy, you're looking better. I mean, that night, that night of your wreck, I didn't know what to think was going to happen to you. I mean, how you were going to turn out." Almost with charismatic insult or a good jab to remind me he adds, "You were totally messed up."

Looking at this guy, I don't know what to think or what connection to make with him. It's that feeling again, like I am supposed to know him, but how? My recall isn't there. I mean, he's definitely not family, standing six feet, two inches, with wavy brown hair, and brown eyes. Now with me having a feeling of absolute truth that we're not related, I'm quizzing myself to figure out who he is.

With perfect timing, Katie jumps in. "Since I didn't have a car when the hospital called me to identify you, Kris was the first person I dialed. I mean, I knew it was a Monday night, so I thought you two would be together. I called him to see if he was hit too, you know, with you in the accident. But when he answered the phone, I told him what happened and how we needed to get to Saint Mary's."

Lifelines

Quickly, I look at Kris for some reaction, and instead of him looking at me for some type of confirmation, his eyes quickly dart to the floor. Hmm. I'm only wondering what all this means.

"I wanted to see how you turned out," Kris blurts out, quickly covering his own blunder for his recovery. "I mean, how you're doing" are the only words coming to his reprieve, only increasing my curiosity.

Another checkup? Another doctor to see? The road trips as car rides for everyone else are now getting old for me.

"Peg, we need to go see Dr. Johnson."

Which makes me take a huge gulp, almost knocking me out of breath. "To see Dr. Johnson again?" I just saw him at the hospital for my leg and the surgery. What could he want now? Hoping this time, it could be for the good.

Peggy Kohlmeyer

"Ben, good to see you again. Peggy, you, too." Dr. Johnson greets us as he walks into the examination room of his office.

Feeling that this is for a simple checkup or update on my condition, I'm feeling comfortable enough to ask, "Dr. Johnson, I know I missed it this year, I mean the Peachtree Road Race in Atlanta, but what are my chances of running it next year? Next summer?"

Having Kris visit reminded me of the run that he had completed and the coveted T-shirt that he earned at the end. I knew if he had completed a 10K run through parts of Buckhead in Atlanta, Georgia, it's something I had to do too. I needed a goal. I mean, walking to the kitchen was a personal success, but now I wanted something more. Let me run. Let me not have Kris one up on me. I have to do this run to even the score.

Lifelines

Pulling me back into his office and the matter at hand, "Peg, let's just see if you can walk again," is the shocking response Dr. Johnson adds, plummeting my heart toward the hopes of completing any goal.

Walk again? Walk again? See if I can walk again? What is he talking about? His statement isn't making any sense. I just can't get his comment to register. Only now having a new sense of immense fear.

Placing the clipboard on the hook his assistant turns a button on a hand held electric saw. *Bzzzzzzzzzzz.* Trying to make my connection, having to focus to what is going on, she's got a saw, maybe even a chain saw to cut. But cut what? My only thought is she is going to cut, cut something. Oh, my gosh…she is going to cut my leg off! She walks toward me as my fear grows. She's walking toward my left leg that's up on the examination

table. No, no, she can't. My dad's here; she can't cut

my leg off. My eyes dart back and forth: the saw,

Daddy, and then back to the saw.

Looking toward Daddy for answers. He

grabs my hand. "Peg, just sit still. She's only cutting

your cast off."

Questioning what he means by that, I only

grip Daddy's hand until she's finished. Gasping for

air, finally I inhale and start to breathe again.

Stepping forward, Dr. Johnson breaks it

apart and separates the cast that I've been wearing

on my left leg. My eyes dart back and forth again,

but this time from my leg to Dr. Johnson. I'm

looking at his face for reassurance or reading his

expression as to what he might do next. Looking

down at my leg, I see what's been covered for the

last four months. That's where it's been. Those are

my toes, and yes, that's my knee, so that's the part that has been hiding from me.

"Daddy, what's up with that?" I ask him, pointing to my calf and shin that hasn't been shaved.

"Peg let's say out of sight out of mind, but you'll have to take care of that when you get home."

I'm looking like I'm a hybrid from *Planet of the Apes*, smiling, realizing that I've made Daddy chuckle with my comment while trying to cover my embarrassment of my unshaven leg.

Stepping toward me again, Dr. Johnson places his left hand gently on the top of my foot. With his right one, he reaches down to a steel tip, almost at a point, that is coming out of the top, below my toes. With me making the connection. "Oh, so that's what itched," I say to myself, as deliberately, Dr. Johnson begins to pull and tug on this pin.

This is something that I can't stand. I can't tolerate it. *Oh, my gosh*, looking down as he's pulling the eight-inch pin out of my left foot. I'm feeling something, but I don't know what it is. I'm not making the connection, and he keeps pulling on that same pin, and pulling, and pulling. My bottom lip is now trembling, and my whole body is quivering. How can he do this to me? What did I ever do to him to deserve this? This feeling, what is it?

As Dr. Johnson reaches the end of the pin, I make the connection, this is *pain*. I'm not sure what to do. I'm not sure how to react to pain this severe that I haven't ever consciously felt. The smell that hits me next makes me cringe. That smell even makes my stomach turn. Making the connection now, I'm smelling my own flesh as he lays down this metal pin.

Reality again hits me. Yes, something has happened to me. Something bad, really bad. To run? To do the Peachtree Road Race? Echoing through my mind with his statement, "Let's just see if you can walk again." Now I only question my own self what *I can* do, not what I can do *again*.

Not even having time to collect myself, Dr. Johnson's hand is resting on my foot. Following his eyes, I see the other pin sticking from the left side of my foot. *Humph*, I should have known that was there, I tell myself, and with no time to prepare, he begins to pull this second one out. No, I'm not ready, but knowing this feeling of pain caused with the action of his hand. "*Arrrrrrhhh*" is what I let out almost as payback to him, shouting from the bottom of my gut.

"Oh, my gosh!" A fellow assistant runs in.

"What's wrong?" I hear from another.

"Who's hurt?" from the third.

"Should I call nine-one-one?" the front office receptionist asks.

The responding nurses are running from the rest of the offices into the room. Dr. Johnson, looking at the assisting nurse who was initially in the room, drearily shares, "You forgot her Novocain."

My only thought? Dr. Johnson, I challenge you on that "Let's see if you can walk again."

The following week, "Peg, you're going to spend some time here, and I just want you to feel comfortable." Dr. Avant greets me at his office with his warm smile. I'm still in a wheelchair to

Lifelines

make my entry easier, but as I enter his last examination room, at the very end of the hallway, I am feeling comfortable already. My favorite color of forest green is painted on the walls, and I think that it's a great coincidence. Looking at the examination chair, "How am I going to get there?" I actually ask out loud, since by this time I'm fully aware of my limitations with my mobility.

Swoosh is the sound of my sweatpants making against the vinyl seat as Dr. Avant lifts and places me.

"Peg, don't let me be able to do that for too much longer."

"But I never thought I would have to think about gaining weight" is my only response.

"Open…. close, yes, that's right, once again, open and close. I see where we're going to have to start. Following the mold that I made of your mouth last week, I've made your partial. This is only a temporary fix until your permanent bridge is ready. This partial will cover the front gap where your left central incisor, left lateral incisor, and your left canine teeth were knocked out. Since your supporting bone or jaw was also affected or knocked in, your bridge is going to have to have the support by your right central incisor, right lateral incisor, and right canine teeth."

Front gap? That's a nice way to put it. Finally having the courage to look at my own mouth, it isn't the missing teeth that I've noticed so much, but it's the gap making up the left side of my upper jawline. It's as if I were in one major fight and I totally lost that round. I can almost place my fist through this hole, and then this is part of my face. An embarrassing but truthful reason for me not to smile. Dr. Avant continues trying to add the positive:

Lifelines

"Looking at your dental X-rays, five teeth were not damaged. You lost the three in the front of your bite, but also a molar and second bicuspid on the lower level of your right side. The others were only partially chipped, and your back molar is cracked in half."

Five teeth? I only have five teeth that were undamaged? When is enough, enough?

"Peg, you're so fortunate to be alive," he adds, noticing my body slump, expressing my desolation. "With the work that's going to be done, what would you like to add to have the smile that you have earned?"

"Hmm," I actually say, letting Dr. Avant know that his invitation is a thought that I'm actually thinking. "Longer teeth. I don't mean like a rabbit, and not buck teeth out front, but longer all over. So when I do smile, people can see my teeth more than all gums." Since my teeth always seemed too small, I've never been really comfortable with my smile.

"I see what you're saying, like adding two centimeters to each one in length, especially in the front." When I nod my head in agreement, he adds, with his heartwarming grin, "Peg, when we're finished, you will truly have a million-dollar smile."

My next road trip is to see an oral surgeon. I'm feeling fortunate with all the recent visits, since these are the doctors Daddy knows. The oral surgeon and dentist I've seen before, so they are my doctors, too. Visiting this same oral surgeon who took my wisdom teeth out, it's more of a comfortable familiar feeling going back to his office, even if it's to have my back cracked molar removed. Is this considered surgery again? How

Lifelines

does it count if it's taking place in the office? I mean, I'm put to sleep for this, with Daddy making sure this time I get the Novocain.

It seems like a weekly visit now, since I'm back to Dr. Avant's office. Today I'm getting my partial. Walking into the front of his office, I'm guiding myself along the secure items in the reception room. Moving from the front door to the back of the first chair and then the edge of the wall.

Looking up, the receptionist grins at me. "Great job, Peg. You can walk yourself down to your room." It's great that she noticed me, and hey, didn't she say, "your room?"

Sliding into the chair, I see that Dr. Avant realizes my grin, since I'm making the *swoosh* noise myself. I'm successfully taking a seat into his dental chair.

Peggy Kohlmeyer

"I never thought about sound effects, Peg." Grinning, Dr. Avant pulls the examination light down to see how my oral surgery went. "Great job. Now a good surprise."

I can't see it, but as the partial is placed in my mouth, I feel like I'm only wearing a retainer again, like I had after my braces. Dr. Avant says the words I'll always hear: "Open…close, yes, that's right. Once again, open…and close," and then handing me a handheld mirror.

Looking at myself, I'm astonished. "Wow, I have teeth."

"Yes, but that's the start. You're to wear this during the day, but make sure you take it out every night. When you brush your teeth, you'll also need to brush your partial, and this is the container where it can rest."

Lifelines

Later that week, Kris asks "So, would you like to go? It's my grandfather's birthday, and you won't be on the spot. People have been asking about you, and now that you're back together, it's a good time to show people how far you've come." Kris rushes nervously through his invitation.

Seeing his body language gives me the idea that he's genuine with his request. Thinking before I answer and going over in my mind with what he's just said, "now that you're back together," makes me wonder what he thought of me before. Is this the reason he's coming by the house more? Is this also the reason that he stayed away? I mean, am I easier to look at? And with me going to his grandfather's birthday, is it only that he wants to show me off?

He breaks my thoughts with his comment. "I know you probably don't have much to wear." I look at him with puzzlement; he quickly corrects himself.

"I mean, the sweatpants around the house and to your doctor's appointments are the best, but I'll take you shopping for an outfit." An outfit? He just said an outfit and shopping? Boy, I do think I might like this guy again.

"We don't have anything smaller than a size two, but when you wear this sash, it'll take up the excess fabric. After you've put on a little weight, these shorts will still fit," the sales associate says.

A size two? I've never worn a size two in my life. I'm five feet, ten inches and wearing a size two; this is truly model thin. How crazy will I seem if I sound a little too excited about this size?

The idea of me waltzing out of the fitting room is a great idea, but it won't happen. I still have to hold on to permanent things to get where I'm going: the wall, the door, a chair, but only with someone sitting on it to stabilize it. Try as I may,

Lifelines

Kris's eyes look up as I thump, glide, thump, glide as my new stride with only my right leg in a long cast, coming out of the dressing room for his approval.

"Wow, those colors look great on you!" A truly coined phrase, but even from him, it's as good as it'll ever get.

Driving back to Athens today is that much more thrilling than it's usually been. I mean, no matter what or when, going back to Athens is always going to be going back home. Athens, Georgia, is where I grew up. This drive is even better. Daddy's with me. No, it's not to go to a UGA football game or for Daddy to hand Katie and me back over to Mom. This is a first time. It's only Daddy and me.

I feel pretty neat now since I'm getting more agile on my feet, or more correctly, more agile on my foot and cast. The step, slide move now comes more easily. Entering into another doctor's office is never a surprise. It's who Daddy is, and it's usually who his friends are. Today, our drive to Athens is to see a doctor for me, and I'm overwhelmed. I also feel tricked since it's after we leave Columbus that I find out the reason for this trip is for me.

Dr. Creagh is a dental specialist. I don't know if he's read the articles about me in the Athens *Banner Herald* newspaper and contacted Daddy or if Daddy contacted him, but I'm here. Yes, another visit to another doctor and more outpatient surgery. In-office surgery is the term I use now, which I'll take anytime instead of having to go back to the hospital.

Dr. Creagh's office is like the others: stuffy on the inside or waiting area, but it loosens up in the patient examination rooms. When Daddy and I walk back, Dr. Creagh is sitting down waiting on us. This is strange, since usually the assistant or nurse checks the record, and then the doctor visits the room. Nope, not today. No assistant to do a meet and greet, but he's right here, waiting in the room for me. For a moment, for an instant, I almost feel like a celebrity.

Standing up to shake each other's hands. "Thanks for your drive, Ben." Which opens the flood of conversation to find the reason for our visit.

"Oh, you're welcome. I feel we're the fortunate ones to participate in your theory of a concrete-based solution mixed with the blood of the patient."

Hearing what Daddy's saying causes me to almost drop to the floor. Theory? Cement and blood? Patient? Now hearing all three, I'm totally aghast. No time even to catch my breath.

"Peg, as you heard, Dr. Creagh has a new dental theory, and he's invited you to participate as the first candidate."

What? I'm the first candidate? He's saying that it's going to be me?

"Yes, Peggy, you have the opportunity to have the outcome of your procedure placed in the monthly edition of *Oral Surgeons*, but just as important, at Emory University in Atlanta. It will go into the student textbook that I'm advising," Dr. Creagh responds reassuringly.

"Oh" is all I can say, which recently seems like my only answer.

"Peg, Peg, it's time to go home." Gosh, now how many times have I heard that?

"Ben, just make sure that she doesn't put her partial back until tomorrow. For success, the cement has to set and the pressure from wearing it would not allow that. I've contacted Dr. Avant, and he'll follow up tomorrow."

"Hey, Peg, it's a success. You're going to be a celebrity with dental students who know your smile," Daddy tells me, and yes, now I know our drive to Athens is totally worthwhile.

"Kris? Oh hey. Lunch? Sure, but do you know what that means? I mean, I appreciate your invitation, but I've got braces on again. Yes, I had to go back to Dr. Lane. These braces are really weird, too. I mean I have the stick-on kind on my front teeth, and then some are also glued to my partial to make it look like it's part of my mouth."

"So you're telling me you didn't have to get any brackets?" Kris questions.

"Brackets? You mean the full band around the tooth?" I ask to confirm his question.

"Yeah" is the common agreement I hear from him. "You bet, but they're only on my teeth in the back."

"How much did this one hurt? I mean, after all you've been through…the accident, the surgery, your bones, your face?"

When he lists it all like that, what can I say, thinking about it. "No, it didn't really hurt. I mean, the front braces just stick to the tooth, sticking to my partial at that. They don't go all the way around."

Getting back to the reason for his call, "So what about lunch?" Kris asks again.

"Lunch? The part about lunch is the fifty-one rubber bands that I'll have to take off when I eat."

"Fifty-one rubber bands?" Kris asks to

confirm.

"Yes, fifty-one. And no, I don't know how to put them on. The colors of the bands help since they cross over trying to reset my bite."

"What else—I mean, what's wrong with your bite? I mean, your jaw was wired together, wasn't it?"

"Yes, but my jaw recessed too far, and they're to realign my jaw again. It's also pretty neat, from what my X-ray shows. I've got a staple or ring in my chin to pull my jaw back together, to hold my bone in place for it to heal."

"A staple?"

"Yes, a staple is what they used."

"Can you see it? I mean, does it show?"

"See it? No, I mean, it's in my chin. It's on the inside of my mouth. Hang on, do you still want to me to go?"

Peggy Kohlmeyer

"Peg, your turn comes next week," Daddy says, walking inside from the garage.

"How's that fair that she gets exempt from all three of her PE classes? I mean, I had to take them." Katie's wailing greets Daddy. With him not even responding to her with his stern discerning look, he casually lays his keys down on the side bar in the kitchen. "Your three physical education class hours are now substituted with a five-hour expressionist of the twenty-first century art class. And your computer class is still a computer class, only with a different course number."

"But why doesn't she have to take PE?" Katie shouts out again. "I mean I did, and I hated it."

With his wry smile, shaking his head: "Katie, just think...PE classes?" while looking directly at me.

Lifelines

Her eyes follow his eyes as she replies, "Oh yeah, I see." Only reassuring me of the terrible image I must present.

No, it isn't the University of Georgia, but Columbus State University is small enough for me not to get lost but big enough that I won't know anyone. All my friends have gone back to UGA anyway. They're off finishing their last semester, or even more, they've already graduated this past summer. Boy, I'm really going to have to catch up. It's as if I'm the only one here, so I can focus. No one will see me, no one I know. I'll blend in, but having a cast going all the way up my hip on my right leg makes me stick out in any crowd.

As Linda, my stepmom, helps me out at the main building, I realize that she's parked in a handicap space. Tomorrow, this can't happen. I

Peggy Kohlmeyer

don't want *that* attention as I get to school. Even worse, to make it to my next class, I have to ride in a golf cart. Now I see the reason to wear a hat to cover my head!

Picking up the phone, "Hey, Kris, yes, classes are OK. No, I don't know anyone. I like computer science the best. Yes, three or four of the school's golf team are there. Lunch is still on tomorrow? After my classes? Sure, you're going to save Linda a trip. She won't have to come back to Columbus State to pick me up." Nervously, I'm thinking of eating in public with Kris seeing what it's like for me to eat. Fifty-one rubber bands, taking off all these stupid rubber bands. All these stupid rubber bands only to eat.

"I wanted to show you, but I'm not sure if you're ready or not." With the lunchtime buzz at the counter of the Dinglewood Pharmacy, I'm not sure what Kris wants to show me but not to show me in public. "I'll just wait until you're more back on your feet. It's pretty, though. It's over a carat," he adds with a hint of tease in his eyes. Now I'm puzzled, struggling to remove the blue rubber band that crosses diagonally from the upper portion of my mouth. We're eating lunch, and Kris is talking about carrots. How in the world would I ever eat a carrot, and why can't he show me a carrot in public? How can he judge if I am ready or not ready? I mean, if I'm not going to eat it.

Back to Dr. Johnson's again? Any visit to his office I do not welcome, even when it says "Welcome" on his front office doormat. No X-rays, no office drama, but with this visit I'm relieved hearing the buzz of the saw, since I know today I am going to get the big cast off my right leg.

Bzzzzzzzzz. With the same assistant going up the right side of the cast and then down the left, I'm holding my breath for the chance of pain, but this time instead it's a gift. I'm getting my cast off, and I'm ready to have it open to see my surprise. "Wow, talk about one hairy leg," I think to myself, but also so white without any sun for four months.

Looking up at Dr. Johnson as he slowly slides the cast from my leg, I'm thinking of all my other parts that still need to get fixed. I slightly grin as elation enters my mind. I realize that, except for my teeth with Dr. Avant, I'm pretty much finished. I'm done. It's over. All the doctor appointments are finished. The rest of it is up to me.

Back at home. "Katie, will you help me with this one?"

"OK, what with?"

Lifelines

"A carrot is what you eat?

"Yes, so?"

"So, the other day when I had lunch with Kris, why did he say that he had a carrot that he wanted me to see?"

"Now, wait, he said that he had a carrot for you?" I hear her responding with curiosity.

Answering, "Yes, and we're not even eating a salad."

"Peg, did he say carrot the one you eat or karat the one in a diamond?"

"We were at lunch; so why would it be a karat in a diamond? I mean, what would I do with a diamond?"

"*A ring*! A diamond ring! Before your accident, you dated forever, like over two years. He's going to give you a diamond ring!"

Peggy Kohlmeyer

"I don't know, I mean, he looked at me hesitating, almost shaking his head, and said I wasn't ready, not ready yet." Puzzlement is now in my head.

"Peg, what does he expect? I mean, look at what you've been through."

Chapter 15
Clarity

Getting an envelope in the mail with a
return address from UGA is at first a surprise,
then confusion. I'm not understanding what's
going on. My mind gets a gray cloud covering my
brain. This haze and confusion is pretty much the
norm for me now. Looking at the envelope,
questioning, "Why did I get anything from them?"
I follow the process that I've established: 1) Look
at it. 2) Think about it. 3) See what connection is
made, and if all those fail? 4) Ask.

Yes, the information is addressed to me,
and yes, it's from UGA, but I didn't attend any
classes this past semester because of my accident.
Why am I getting this? Waiting, thinking,
deliberating. "Katie?"

"Right here."

"How come this is addressed to me? From the University of Georgia?

"I don't know; did you open it?"

"Oh" is my only answer since really, I should've known that.

Looking directly at the right-hand side under the title "Grade Earned," listed in a column is WF, WF, WF, and WF, representing withdrawal/fail for each of the summer class that I enrolled. Only having the "What?" question enter my mind; the trembling of my bottom lip takes control. I'm mentally digesting what I've done, or even more, what I've failed to do.

"Peggy? What is it? What's wrong?" Katie asks, taking the summer grades out of my hand. "This is only showing that you were enrolled in these classes, but you withdrew," with a question in her voice, showing that she doesn't understand what I'm seeing.

Sucking in some air to breath while I'm trying to talk, "No, no, that's not all, it's saying W/F, withdrawal/*fail.* It's saying that I've failed all my classes, Katie, all my summer classes." I've never ever failed at anything, at any of my classes. Triggering a wisp of a memory in my mind of class grades, turns into a flickering thought and its importance building into a meaning. I'm remembering that anything below a B grade means to Daddy that we simply aren't trying hard enough. At the same time, I'm also remembering my envy for how much harder I've always had to try to impress my dad with my grades. Grades that come so easily for Katie, who is standing next to me, who doesn't even understand what failure means.

Peggy Kohlmeyer

Holding my grades again in my hand, looking at what I didn't do. Again, I recognize that something really has happened to me. This something that's happened is not only physical, which everyone can see, but also mental. I mean, with my brain. Now I understand. This is another something I have to fix.

I'm going to say that Columbus State University in Columbus, Georgia, is where I've had a revolving or even rotating door. Exactly the same school that I initially attended on a trial basis to have Daddy's permission to go to the University of Georgia. Remember? I was sixteen and basically dropping out of high school to get there. Now I've got so much more to prove, and it's going to be harder. This time, I'm starting without anything, and I'm not talking about the paper diploma to represent high school. I'm going back without anything, like a blank slate in my brain, as I'm still focusing on regaining the simple things like my own common sense of turning on a light switch.

Columbus State University opens its door for me again as a transient student. The graduation requirements for me are the same as they were at UGA. I still have the computer science class, but now it's even more intense, as Internet information is surging daily. Art Expressionists is my elective course, but it's more difficult than I ever thought. How do I know what an artist is thinking when they created their masterpiece? How do I know what they're feeling? For me I'm only trying to make these daily connections myself. And the physical education classes? I'm glad I'm exempt and not taking them, since every day I start with the *ump* I have to make getting my body out of bed.

My daily to-do list now only holds the major items for me to accomplish. Grinning, since I remember to do the daily basics of personal upkeep and hygiene, like washing my face and brushing my teeth. Sure, I've learned from my mistakes, but this is where I wish there was a book. For me I need a guidance book to give me the answers I don't know, and I'm too embarrassed to ask.

Starting with breakfast, I'm really trying to understand this whole idea. I mean, it's relatively simple since it's pretty much in the name. This morning meal breaks the fast, since the previous meal happened the night before at dinner time. I start with what to eat as my daily question. This morning, frustration is bumped by how do I eat it? With all the rubber bands on my braces to take off, simple and easy are the new mottos of my life. This is followed with the reminder of the facial scar where my chin and lip were reattached. Placing my partial into my mouth brings me back to the idea of food. What to eat for breakfast though? My new mantra in life is refocusing directly to the point at hand, so breakfast is something that tastes good and is easy. Finally finding the agreement between crushed frosted flakes and peanut butter.

Overlooking my right collarbone sticking out a little more than the left and only a slight gimp in my right leg, which is shorter than my left leg, my self-improvement plan continues. Physically, by sight I'm pretty much up to par. Not the best, but far better than what I was before. Getting my braces off, helping my bite realign, and my teeth replaced with a permanent bridge mark my final steps. This means

Peggy Kohlmeyer

my dental appointments with Dr. Avant are coming

to an end.

"OK, Peg, open, close…once again, open,

close." Dr. Avant's handing me a handheld mirror.

Tell me what you think."

Looking directly into the mirror at my

reflection and seeing my eyes, it's that reassurance

it's me. Quickly questioning myself how long I've

been sitting in his dental office, five months, six

months, now up to a year? Hesitating with my

reflection in the mirror, I see my nose. Slowly

moving my eyes down, I see the top of my lip;

hesitantly peeking, I see my new teeth that make up

my new mouth and my new smile.

"Dr. Avant, it's beautiful. They're beautiful."

Looking again at my smile in the mirror, it or rather

my new teeth don't seem real. Do they really

belong to me?

Lifelines

"A million-dollar smile is what you deserve, and with your patience, I didn't want you to feel disappointed."

Disappointed? "Oh, Dr. Avant, I could have never guessed. They're longer, they're whiter, my smile is just so much bigger. It's even better than my old smile. But how do I keep them this white?"

"Since they're not yours, not your real teeth, stay away from red wine, tea, or colas."

He's saying to stay away from iced tea and Coke? "For how long?"

"As long as you want them to stay white." This is simple. I can follow these guidelines.

Completing my internship and gaining a full-time position in retail management, I've done it. I've earned my college degree, but with the timing of my birthday in January and the

Peggy Kohlmeyer

internship lasting until March, overall, I'm simply crushed. I've earned my Bachelor of Science home economics degree, and I'm four months behind in meeting my number one goal. I turned twenty-one. Others say that I'm fortunate to make it to this birthday and be of legal age, only dropping my mouth open in disbelief when someone says, "Let's celebrate, let's go have a drink!"

Time as always passes, and two years in retail management gives me the stability that I've needed to find myself. Not knowing what specific areas of my brain were affected, it's a guessing game as to who or what gets the bad luck in what I've mistakenly said or done. I mean, at times I'm walking around in a daze, having that gray cloud blocking my thinking. This cloud isn't the blame or

Lifelines

excuse, but without me making the simple connections, result in my social comments or blunders. These I regret instantaneously realizing I've said them out loud. Having the established routine of my job, my brain mentally gets back on par.

Then on one day, it's almost as if this entire fog for me is gone. The sun is brighter, the fluorescent store lighting is stronger, and I'm realizing that minute, that hour, and that day, retail isn't what I want to do. Yet what? There's not a book to find any of life's daily directions. I only know that there is something more for me somewhere.

Then it hits me. I made it a point of returning to Saint Mary's Hospital in Athens, Georgia, to express my thanks and gratitude for everyone who helped me. At first I wasn't going to make a

Peggy Kohlmeyer

personal visit. Initially, I wanted to write everyone a thank-you note or card. A card for everyone from my countless physicians, the EMTs, the nurses, the secretary at the reception desk, the custodian who has to keep a hospital clean, and the data entry clerk for keeping all records updated, and then there is the actual medical staff from my X-rays, to my nutrition, to the front office clerk drugs, and the actual surgeons. Do you know how many thank-you notes that would've meant for me to write? And at this time, too, I couldn't even lift a pen. I couldn't forget any of the staff, since all their jobs are important.

Making it a point to visit Saint Mary's wasn't what I thought it should be. Only a few people were on duty, and I left feeling personally empty. I hadn't had the opportunity to express my true gratitude. Leaving disillusioned and carrying the question with me: how do I say thanks to all those who took care of me?

This one day, it strikes me.

On this one day, the lights are brighter. I'm even having more clarity about my purpose. I answer the question that's been nagging me *why I didn't die*, but why I'm still alive. Building on this, I figure it's simple. I'm going to watch after *them*. I'm going to pay it forward for everyone who has a connection to me and express my thanks.

Simple now, I've got to teach. I'm going to teach those kids of today who are our future tomorrow. For those whom I'll educate will look after those who looked after me. I'm thanking them with those of tomorrow since the students I teach are our future. Teaching them will prepare them for us while thanking the adults who took care of me.

Peggy Kohlmeyer

Calling it my "light bulb" that's turning back on somewhere, Kris gets this message, too. I don't know if it's me having to think about myself first and not extend myself to him. I don't know if it's because I'm labeled "a few steps behind" while still trying to figure out the simple things, but I do know that when Katie says, "Oh, he gave that diamond to your ex-roommate," I only let out a big sigh, not with disappointment, but almost with relief.

For me whether it's my naiveté, gullibility, or plain stupidity, finding out that Kris is playing a game, stringing me along, acting like he's interested in me for some money that I didn't get. I don't know if Kris's karat idea of marrying me was to marry a millionaire.

His interest almost immediately stops after the drunk driver who hit me takes his own life rather than returning to jail. When you can't claim money from a corpse, our lawsuit is dropped. Here I feel someone somewhere is truly looking after me. I'm so lucky it's an ex-roommate who falls for him and gets a carrot that you can't eat in a ring instead of me. To further support this, I never hear from him again when he knows there isn't any law settlement involved.

Refocusing on my life, Clarke Middle School is a school I've known since it's in Athens, Georgia. It's my old school that I attended for sixth, seventh, and eighth grade, but my problem is that I really don't know much of what happened to me there. It's my gray category of what I can't recall. I don't have many memories of those three years, except for two teachers: Mrs. Little for sixth grade English, introducing me to the stems, prefixes, and suffixes, with the word *monotone*. *Mono* for one and *tone* for sound, meaning *one sound*. And Mrs. Brinson for seventh grade science. She had us get out of desks and rotate like the planets, and I volunteered as Jupiter because of my size. Remembering these two teachers with what my memory and "noggin" have been through, I feel these two teachers truly made an impression on me. This is the reason that I'm making the decision that when I teach, it's in these so-called middle grades. I mean, if I can remember them, then I'll reciprocate and make some type of positive impression for the children I'll teach.

As always seeing Daddy at his office conveys the importance of our conversation. Seeking his approval in earning my postgraduate educational degree, he seems to challenge my decision when he remarks, "Peg, do you know that what I make in a month, you'll make in a year as an educator?" His statement doesn't shake me. The nervous reaction of my bottom lip quivering does set in as I reply, "Daddy, that's not the reason that I want to teach."

"Peg, when I was in the second grade, my teacher had a weekly contest of who would read the most. She charted it out with airplanes for the books that we've read. When my plane was the highest, I got the weekly trinket or prize." Captivated and listening, biting back my lip so I won't cry. He continues, "She's the reason that I took education more seriously."

Always in awe of my dad, looking at the degrees and awards smothering his office walls while refocusing on him, he completely startles me after what he's just shared, "Peg, this could be the best decision you've ever made."

Yet smiling back at him as I remind him, "No, Dad, putting my seat belt on is the best

Peggy Kohlmeyer

decision I've ever made." with Daddy chuckling at that.

Saying the third time's a charm and returning again to Columbus State University, this time is different, too. This time it's all about me. Going to college this time is different. This time I'm very serious. Not that I wasn't serious the first time, but now, since it's tuition that I have to pay, the academics are the focus. Finding out all my options. The educational foundation classes and student teaching that I have to complete are categorized as post graduate, since I have the BSHE degree. These I take as a regular college student during the day. Already having an undergraduate degree, I can seek a graduate degree at night. Labeling it as another two-for-one program, I'm working on two separate degrees at the same time with the emphasis on cost effectiveness.

Making my huge career move and needing job security, I research the areas for the teachers who are needed most. Finding out that it's in the areas of math and science further motivates me to label these two as the major and minor areas for my middle grades degree. My rationale for selecting these two areas to concentrate on is that I loved science when I was in the seventh grade, and math left me puzzled. If it was hard for me when I was that age, I have to make it easier for my future students to learn.

My classes start with graduate school. Remembering and following a Daddy-ism: being on time is five minutes early. To him showing up on time is late. A graduate class? I'm there fifteen minutes ahead of class time. Call me or label me the goober that I am, on my first day of graduate school, I'm the first to show up for class. Sitting in the front row, in the center seat, time is passing, and seats are filling up.

The professor is speaking, and almost every seat in the lecture hall is filled. It's more than five minutes into class that the last student walks in. The only empty seat is located next to me. Beautifully grinning, a girl fills this chair, and we're both respectfully attentive to the professor as he explains his expectations to pass his course. Finishing up his closing and turning for clarity, this late-class-entry girl next to me with blond hair and blue eyes gently asks me, "I'm not going to make the next two classes. I have to go skiing." Here, I actually gulp as she continues, "Can I borrow your notes that I miss?"

Lifelines

What? is the only thing I can think of her request. She's late to class and is asking to borrow my notes? What gall, what nerve, so of course my remark is, "Oh, no problem."

When she returns from her trip, I give Susanne a copy of my notes. The best notes that she's ever received, since I made sure they were the best notes I'd ever taken to prove something to myself, if not to her. *What?* Is all I ask myself when she outscores me on our first test. This is how our fantastic friendship begins.

Susanne is like me. She's already got one degree, finance, and is getting another, with post-graduate classes in the morning and graduate classes at night. Keeping up with each other since we're both seeking the license of middle grades education, we have core classes together. It turns into an unwritten competition that goes on for us, or rather

Peggy Kohlmeyer

for me. I have to gain back my pride and beat her on a test. Any test. After a semester of classes, I find out that her trip skiing was to chaperone her two kids, not the blond bunny trip that I thought she had taken. Within the year, she's the life mentor that I need.

Chapter 16
Coffee?

Huntersville is in North Carolina. Nope, I'd never heard of it before either. I think it's like one of those cities that gains its recognition because it becomes a suburb of a larger city, when the city itself grows. A great comparison is Gwinnett County in Georgia, which is beautiful in name and from my understanding a great place to live, but it really didn't gain attention for itself until Atlanta, Georgia outgrew itself. The city of Atlanta was the city proper, taking up Fulton County. Today if you say Atlanta, people definitely know that it's in Georgia, but they can be talking about Cobb County (Marietta), Gwinnett County (Lawrenceville), or Dekalb County (Decatur). Atlanta's grown so much in population, it's like it overflowed into those surrounding counties but still wants the bragging rights of living in the capital city and claiming it as home. My point? Huntersville is known, since it's a suburb of Charlotte, North Carolina. Moving here almost twelve years ago, I have to mention Charlotte for people to know where in North Carolina I live. Saying Huntersville now, people have an idea, since the city itself has grown.

"Before we go to the gym, I want to go by Belk's and check their running shoes. Get this, their New Balance are like thirty dollars off!" ecstatically Mike, my boyfriend requests. Since his work schedule keeps him away most of the time, how can I not agree? When he's home, the time that we spend together is valued, even if it's doing his errands.

Meeting Mike is not the end of my story, but the beginning. I mean, I've never, ever thought I'd meet and deserve somebody like him. My grandmother Mimi tells me that I've always settled for less than the best, less than what I deserve. "Peg, if someone bats an eyelash at you, your game. You're so into them, and then you get lost. You become what they want and not who you are, and you, you're a pretty remarkable girl."

Serious relationships for me? I've been through a few. It's when I'm tired of being what they want me to be rather than me as myself that I save the emotional hassle, and I step out and leave. I want to do the leaving rather than being the one who is left. Yes, eventually this makes me pretty cold, perhaps, in other people's eyes.

The irony with Mike is he's actually always leaving me every time he goes to work. His rotation is on for seventeen days and off for ten. Sharing a work ethic similar to mine, respect, understanding, and support toward one another places our relationship greatly above par. He argues that it's eleven days that he's off, but since it's a travel day for him going back to work, I don't see how this can count since we're not together. Having him home, with only two days to go before he leaves again, you see what I mean when I can't deny his request to go to the mall. Also, with our school system out on winter holiday break, it's easy enough to go with him, rather than me sitting home alone.

Following the newspaper advertisement, the Belk's at Northlake Mall has every New Balance running shoe size, except his. "There are some at the South Park store, and I can have a pair put on hold," the sales associate quickly pipes in.

"Oh, thanks, but we'll just drive down there," Mike says to my chagrin. After working retail for a few years, shopping isn't my favorite pastime, especially during the holidays. My heart goes out to all the mall employees who have the extended holiday hours they work.

Arriving at Belk's at the South Park Mall, after the twenty-two-mile drive, I notice that time is starting to crunch and pass away. It's not that I mind spending it with Mike and helping him find a new pair of running shoes to pack, but our plans were set for the gym. It's not that I live, breathe, and die at the gym, but a missed workout can never be made up. This is the mantra that some say I live by. But then, isn't it the truth? Keeping my positive spirit, it's still early and a down and back trip to the other mall with no flittering around, we can make the gym, which doesn't close until seven.

"What? You don't have my size?" Mike controls his fury. The sales associate does another inventory check and says, "No, sir, Northlake has two pairs; we don't have any." These are the words

I'm hearing, realizing Mike's patience or tolerance is getting tapped, since that is the mall we left to get here. Quickly I interject, "Hey, no problem, we can go back, but this time if you'll call and put them on hold for us," I add to appease the beast, as Mike likes to think of himself.

With our time at this mall done and nearing my desperation mode for afternoon caffeine, I simply ask, "Can we go get some coffee somewhere?" Only thinking we'll do a quick turnaround to one of the coffee shops at South Park. "Sure, I know a great place," Mike says, walking out the front door of the mall, back to his truck.

Huh? With the numerous stores surrounding the mall, I can't think of anyone else that has coffee. Why didn't we go back inside? Instead, we're getting back into his truck and crossing over to a building that's got a very posh restaurant inside. Quickly asking him, "Do you know how much a cup of coffee will cost in there?" as we're entering the building, passing the five-star restaurant on the left-hand side.

"Oh, they've got free coffee," Mike says, as we take the direct right into the diamond store. Totally puzzled, since this entire venture started with a cheap price on a pair of running shoes, and we're now waiting in the foyer for the store's security to buzz us back. Totally dazzled with the brilliance of the store's lights, the glass cases, and the diamonds themselves, I'm following Mike's lead. I'm dumbstruck as the sales associate greets Mike, and she simply asks, "How can I help you?"

"Oh, we'd like to get some coffee."

Getting even more puzzled as her attention quickly darts to me.

Peggy Kohlmeyer

"What kind would you like?"

Knowing that there is no chance of anything other than the basic cream and sugar, I go for the splurge, as almost a test. "The best would be a regular cup of coffee with an additional shot of espresso, sugar-free hazelnut crème, and enough sweetener to cut the bite," realizing that my request is fruitless.

The sales associate turns to Mike; he simply says, "The same."

With her not even giving us a hint of saying no to our request, she adds, "That sounds like a great choice. Why don't you two go ahead and look around while I go fix this up?" and we do, bending over the cases, gazing at the brilliance of the diamonds.

Lifelines

She brings out our coffee, and on the first taste, I blurt out, "Wow, I think this is better than I could even fix."

"That's what we try to do. What exactly are you looking for? Why don't we start with the rings?" Stepping behind the counter, she brings out a blue velvet cloth and motions for Mike and me to take a seat. Beginning with the diamond rings and looking at their brilliance, I'm only gawking at all the lovely stones and ring bands. With perfect timing, she asks me, "Where do you want to start?" This time, not wanting to settle as Mimi says that I've always done in my past, I'm pointing to the most opulent single-stone diamond ring in the far-right-hand corner of the showcase.

Pulling the ring out, "Oh, it's beautiful." She adds, "But is this what you want?"

Peggy Kohlmeyer

I take this as her invitation to fulfill my delusion. Sliding my eyes over at Mike, with him into his coffee, he simply nods his head in agreement.

"Well, actually, a ring with three stones. The larger one in the center, balanced by two smaller stones, one on either side." I begin expressing my dream.

"Oh, I see. I'll be right back." She steps into the back. I'm guessing to take loose stones out of the vault. Seeing the store clock, I'm thinking of how much time we're using up still away from the gym, but then, we are drinking our coffee, and it is for free.

Returning carrying a tray of diamonds, she sits down in front of us behind the display case. "Let's get started with the center-stone first. Let's start with this one," she says, as she points to the one loose diamond stone, placing it on my closed fingers, along the back of on my right hand. I'm looking at it. It's really brilliant and big, but it's just there. It's not doing it for me. I shake my head no, and she picks it up, placing it back in its velvet case.

Moving onto the next stone, she shares, "This one is beautiful," pointing to the second one. With a quick intake of my own breath, almost as if my heart just skipped a beat, my bottom lip starts quivering. How could a stone be so gorgeous? Have so much life and vitality? Stop, wait, what are you doing? Cutting a quick glance again at Mike at my right, I see that he's actually nodding his head in agreement.

"Let's put this one aside but go for the last one to make sure." Now as if a routine, she replaces the second stone in its cloth case. "When is the wedding going to be?"

Peggy Kohlmeyer

Mike grins slightly. "Oh, I haven't asked her yet."

Chuckling at his comment, the sales lady is going to the last stone, "This one is the best of the three," picking it up from the left-hand side of her tray.

Looking down at it, it's the largest stone of all three and has the most dazzle. Looking again at Mike for his input, a gentle shrug from him lets me know it's up to me. This diamond does have more brilliance and radiance than the first two, but for some reason, it's overwhelming, "It's almost gaudy." I sense it's a better fit for some other person. It's not me.

Feeling Mike's sigh of relief, she adds, "Boy, she's right. It's also the most expensive of the three."

Lifelines

Wham! It hits me. How much do these stones cost? How far is Mike going to play this charade game with me? Isn't he done with his coffee yet? Did he forget that the gym closes at seven?

Refocusing on where we are and what's going on, almost in an apology for my comment on the last stone, "No, I mean, it's so beautiful but almost overwhelming for me."

"So, this is an engagement ring?" asks the clerk. "That's a new one. Letting her pick out the ring before you propose." She goes back to the second stone, taking it again from her tray and placing it back on the resting place on my fingers for a second glance.

Propose? Mike's supposed to propose to me? Heck, we're just getting free coffee, and I'm dreaming of a perfect ring. Propose? That means marriage, but even more, if he buys this kind of ring, it means he actually loves me.

"Great. Now to find the stones to enclose it, to compliment it," she says, as she disappears with it into the back area again.

Returning, this time she's got the second center stone that we've selected on the tray, but now with individual clear containers, each with smaller diamonds. Beginning, she opens one container then another and puts one of these smaller stones on either side of the center stone I've selected.

She holds it up for Mike and me to see, "Oh, I see what you mean. That's going to make a beautiful ring."

"Thank you." While expressing my agreement, I shake my head no. That's not the look I want. She replaces those two stones and takes out two more, each from a different, separate container.

"Oh, these two are beautiful," she says, looking at each stone individually. "They have the cut that focuses on the center stone."

Again, she holds up the tray for Mike and me to see. I gasp.
These stones are so pretty they seriously take my breath away.

Noticing my reaction, she says, "Hold out your left hand," and I do so. She places the stones along the breaks of my fingers for me to realize their shine and suddenly, a tear slides down from the corner of my eye. I can't do this, they can't see me, biting back my lip. Cry? The stones are so beautiful, I can't say anything. How can I wear these? How can someone love me so much as to even purchase them? For Mike to buy these for me?

Peggy Kohlmeyer

My bottom lip is totally trembling now, with another single tear sliding down the right side of my face.

Mike looks at me sheepishly, but with a twinkle in his eye, "Oh, that means we'll take 'em."

Realizing that I'm crying over loose diamonds, my embarrassment sets in. Handing me a Kleenex and pointing to another counter across the room, she politely suggests, "Why don't you go look at the wedding bands while Mike and I talk about prices."

Prices? Holy smoke. How serious is this getting?

Nervously looking at the wedding bands, I'm really trying to listen, but I don't really want to hear about the expense or money, thinking about my limited teacher's pay. Waiting for reality to set in, since we only came in for a cup of coffee, and free coffee at that.

Mike and the sales associate approach. She's quickly behind the counter where I'm standing. I've picked out a band for Mike. It's strong but simple. Me? Heck, after what we've just picked out, who says I even need an additional band?

She's writing down information on the same tab as the initial engagement ring. "We'll have to send the loose stones to New York to our designer for a special layout. But picking out the wedding band, did you want white gold or platinum for your setting?"

Knowing the price difference between the two this time, I look at Mike for him to make the decision, and he's grinning.

"Platinum."

Gosh, is he serious about this?

"These bands are in the store, but with the holiday, it will be a week to ten days before we have the engagement ring back. This will give you time to think of any inscription you would like to have placed inside the wedding bands and obtain insurance for the engagement ring."

Insurance? Obtain insurance for a ring that I'm going to wear? When is this dream going to end?

"Insurance covering the full total of karats."

"Does this make me more of a vegetarian?" I nervously reply, thinking of some humor, remembering the last time someone mentioned this and I could only think *carrot.* My mouth suddenly drops open. Yes, the stones are beautiful, and no, I didn't settle, but where's my mind?

Lifelines

"And when you pick them up, don't forget to ask her to marry you, since this is such a gorgeous ring."

"Well, what do you think?" I'm finally asking Mike.

"I think you have some fantastic taste."

"You mean in men?" I say as I grin.

"I hope so, since you're going to marry me." Mike quickly replies.

Reminding him, "But you haven't asked me yet."

"Let's wait until we get the ring." Grinning back.

Sitting next to each other at dinner and giggling over our afternoon event, I ask him, "Do you want to go back and get some more coffee?"

Peggy Kohlmeyer

"No, that's the most expensive free cup of coffee I've ever bought."

"Yeah, but don't forget, we did go back to Northlake and got your shoes." An engagement like this is not to be missed and never, ever copied again, even if we didn't make it to the gym.

Since Mike is someone I'm sure about, meeting in June, engaged in December, and married in May (well, almost married) is not what I consider a rush marriage. Yes, I think Mike and I complement and complete each other with our smiles, our eyes, and our personalities. It's because of his good looks that it took two years of seeing him at our gym for me to drop my protective wall and allow him to say hello. Height? At first glance he's intimidating. His shoulders are broad, and he's muscular in his build, and his height is around six feet, making his overall appearance way taller. College education? With him and by him, I realize that education isn't gained from only going to classes on a college campus. Having his career in the air force, transferring to the commercial airlines and to where he is now, his life experiences far out measure any textbook or class. Meeting Mike, I understand that my previous qualifications were limiting, while I was missing the most important characteristic: respect. It's the respect that he has for me, for what I believe, my work ethic, and my own morality that I hold true.

Marriage to Mike is something that I'm sure about, even waking up on the floor at the Kennedy Airport in New York. We weren't supposed to be here and sleeping on the airport floor I don't think is on anyone's bucket list. We started out this morning at the Charlotte, North Carolina, airport early, I mean really early. Before the ticket agents were even there.

Following the airport guidelines and reading our boarding passes, we have a two-hour wait after checking in for our international flight. We did it, we made it, and boarded at 6:00 a.m., flying to make our connection in Atlanta. In Atlanta, it's a forty-five-minute delay to catch our next flight to the Sandals Resort in Antigua. At Sandals, it's our week for our wedding, followed directly by our honeymoon, earning the catchy name wedding-moon.

This plan seemed great, only the delay in our departure from the Charlotte airport wasn't taken into account. Waiting the extra minutes on the tarmac in Charlotte for clearance to depart puts our arrival late in Atlanta. With us both running to reach the concourse, we're out of breath, feverishly tapping on the Atlanta International window, watching as our Antigua jet pulls away. Standing with exasperation, we're now wondering about our luggage and if it is on that departing plane.

With Mike's work schedule, his time off is always planned. For the years that he's flown out to his work location, his vacation time has not been filled with this much excitement. I remind myself to compliment him on his patience.

Mike's trying to get us on the next flight, explaining to the attendant. She replies, "Wedding? You're going to Sandals Antigua to get married?" The Delta employee smiles as she looks at me holding my wedding dress in the white zipped-up formal bag. Today, this carry-on is as important as the purse with my passport, slung over my left shoulder.

Peggy Kohlmeyer

"Antigua, I've been there, but for your wedding, that's going to be beautiful. Let me see, let me see." As she looks at her computer screen, my eyes are following hers. Wait, her eyes have stopped. I'm holding in my breath, scared of what she's going to say next. "Let's see, we have one flight out a week leaving from here in Atlanta, and that was it. The next weekly flight is from New York, from Kennedy Airport, leaving tomorrow, Sunday."

Kennedy Airport? New York? I've never been there. I mean, it's an opportunity, and we'll still make it to Antigua.

"That's really our only choice?" Mike asks, as I glance at him to my right.

"Yes sir," she simply says.

Lifelines

"And our luggage? Did it make it on the flight we missed, or is it going up to follow us up to New York?"

Scared? Didn't I mention that I was scared in hearing her answer as she responds, "I don't know. You'll just have to check for your luggage when you're at baggage pickup in New York."

The rush we just made to make our Atlanta connection that we missed now leaves us with a five-hour delay, waiting on the next New York flight. It's tedious thinking about our luggage, but that is basically all we can do. Mike has all his clothing for the week and our wedding in his one suitcase, and mine is spread between two. My actual suitcase has my bathing suits, dresses for our evenings, clothing to run and work out, shorts for the days, and the finishing touches for my wedding day. In my second or usual carry-

Peggy Kohlmeyer

on, I've got my makeup, hair dryer, curling iron, and sunscreen in varying SPFs for the beach. Now I'm wondering if they made it on that flight or any flight.

Catching the flight to the New York airport, things seem to be going smoothly, but I'm still having my doubts. Standing at the baggage carousel looking down as the bags pass by, we wait and wait. Nope, our luggage wasn't on our flight. "The next flight from Atlanta, then" is the response Mike gets asking the luggage attendant and for every arriving flight after that. Finally, the last flight lands, and our luggage has to be here.

It's 1:30 a.m., and it has been a long, long day. Both of us are standing looking down as the luggage carousel goes around and around, hopefully holding out for this one last time. Since the carousel is empty, we watch it spin once more

for our own reassurance, finally admitting our
bags are not here.

     This trip was for our wedding. This trip was
for our honeymoon. Things that were so well
planned with so much hope have gone so awry. It's
getting close to 2:00 a.m., and we have to be back at
5:00 a.m. for the two-hour time needed for an
international flight. By the time we leave to find a
hotel to spend the night, how much time would we
actually sleep? Even worse, what if we overslept
and missed our only flight?

     "It's up to you. What do you want to do?"
Mike's leaving this decision to me.

     "We can take turns here sleeping. I mean
there's not any real reason to find a hotel. This
isn't our only opportunity to see New York City.
We can't see anything now, and if we go and find

a hotel, that's only lost time for sleep. Most of all, we have to catch tomorrow's flight."

"Peg, if that's what you want, you sleep first, and thanks."

"Thanks for what?"

"You didn't blow up; you haven't cried. Peg, you haven't turned around to leave."

"Mike, some things I've learned you can't control, like the weather and airline fights, and the best of all, we're here together."

"Thanks Peg, again I'll watch over you, but where, there's only the floor."

The next morning, looking out my airplane window and calling on my positive attitude, I stop and notice the departing radiant cloudless blue sky. As Mike and I are the first passengers on the 8:00 a.m. Antigua flight, after getting a courteous upgrade to first class, I'm getting embarrassed about how I feel, wearing the going-away dress that I put on yesterday at 4:00 a.m. That's also the last time I brushed my teeth. That's the last time I washed my face and applied my make up for that day, or rather yesterday. Realizing I'm feeling pretty icky, wondering how "day old" I must look, since it is the next day.

Having boarded the plane as the first passengers on the flight, we're the first passengers off and into the Antigua airport luggage lobby. We definitely know how the luggage process goes after so many times and hours of our experience in New York. For luggage collection, we stand and look at the spinning carousel. Looking at the luggage that's going around and around, we see the bags that were on our plane. I also see their owners claim them. No, ours are not here, but to be sure again, we wait until the carousel is empty. Finding the attendant to ask, he points to the far corner where rows and rows of luggage stand. Mike, holding back his run but calling it a very brisk pace, shares his excitement. exclaiming "*Yes!*" picking out his bag. What a sense of relief. That can only mean if his is here, my two are around somewhere.

That's it, I see it. It's my tan-and-brown carry-on bag that has all my makeup. Now we've found two of our three luggage pieces and have one to go. I'm looking and looking…and looking. Desperation sets in. Where's my other bag?

Talking to the same Antigua luggage attendant again, Mike asks, "We got off the last Delta flight, and her bag is missing. The other two we found, but we're missing hers."

"Your baggage tags?" the same attendant replies, which Mike quickly presents.

Lifelines

Having my elbows up resting on the Delta counter, I've got a quick reminder of the life lines found in the palm of my hand. Gently tightening each hand into a fist, I'm covering up my palms, not looking at some broken line matching this event.

"Oh, that bag?" Looking up from the computer screen, "It's in route to Jordan…Amman, Jordan."

"Huh?" is my questioning sound.

Arriving one day later at the Sandals resort, it's now thirty-six or more hours that I've been in the same dress without a shower. I'm washing off any lingering remnant of the Kennedy Airport's floor. Feeling so clean and totally refreshed except for the loss of sleep, I can only ask, "Mike do you have anything I can borrow? I mean, to wear?" Both of us realize the need to meet with the wedding planner, since we missed our appointment yesterday.

Peggy Kohlmeyer

"Amman, Jordan, you say?" The Sandals wedding planner asks.

"Yes, that's what the Delta agent said." Mike responds.

I notice her eyes are questioning me wearing Mike's oversize shirt and shorts that I have on. "Do they have any idea when it's supposed to arrive or even worse, will it arrive?" She addresses the worst ideas in my head.

"We do have the baggage tag with the tracking number. We're supposed to check it at the Delta website," Mike confirms.

"With today as Sunday and your wedding scheduled for Wednesday, the next available opening for the ceremony is Friday. That also gives you time for your luggage to get here."

"Thank you, thank you, that's such a relief," I'm saying, since our wedding was the entire reason

Lifelines

for this trip. Starting our marriage with this

experience, it doesn't even matter if it decides to

rain.

Peggy Kohlmeyer

Chapter 17
My Gray Days

Walking into the kitchen blocking the light from my eyes, the brightness still hurts them. Even though it's February and the sun is gone, these bright lights hurt me down to my bones. Looking down the overhead lights' blinding brightness reflects up from our linoleum floor. With fluorescent lighting, there's no way to dim them. It's dinner time and with Mike at work, it's only dinner for one. Once more I'm only fixing a meal for me.

Only me? I can skip this meal. I mean, it's not that I'm even hungry now. Turning, leaving the kitchen away from the lights, I sigh with a sense of relief, or is that my own depression that is settling in again? One step, second step, stopping and thinking, "What about school tomorrow?" Knowing I'll only regret not eating dinner tonight. Turning back around once again, I'm giving up and letting the bright, fluorescent kitchen lights win tonight's internal fight.

Standing in front of the refrigerator with the door open, I'm waiting for something to speak to me, to tell me what I'm having for dinner. This isn't working. Keeping my pledge of not thinking about school when I'm away from school isn't working either. *How is that project going to go? When will I have time to introduce it?* Dinner? What's for dinner? *Tutoring? Oh yeah, tomorrow is Tuesday: Tuesday morning tutoring.* Scramble an egg? With toast? That's a frying pan that I'll have to clean. Salad? I've got the spinach, but what else is going to go in it? Vegetables? My mind turns into a spiral, my thoughts chasing one another. What else can I put in it? *Lee and Malique for Tuesday morning tutoring tomorrow? They'll both be there. Cory? He*

needs to show up, but I can catch him at lunch.
Tracy? She seems to be grasping it in class. OK, a
spinach salad with chicken. *Sam and Gloria always*
show up.

Even with the bright lights of our kitchen, I'm
dropping deeper into my own gloom. *Why did this*
have to happen to me? With a four-block teaching
day and seeing the same thirty-one students first
block and fourth block, somewhere around the third
block, or my planning time, I have to swap from the
internal logical side on the left side of my brain for
Math to my creative, right side of my brain for
English/ Language Arts. Every morning for first
block, labeled as the first eighty-five-minute class
period, using the left side of my brain, I
energetically greet my homeroom class of thirty-one
kids with the math concepts that they have to
master. Second block, or the next eighty-five-minute

Lifelines

class, is a totally new group of students I've inherited when a teaching position wasn't filled, but also for math. Some consider this my easy class, since I'm only repeating what I have already done: review of the basic mathematical foundations, multistep equations, with the basics of algebra and geometry. Fourth block, I teach my first-block kids, but now it's honors language arts. *Wham*, I swap to the right side of my brain in the afternoon. I'm teaching my thirty-one students from the morning Math class to grade-level comprehension in literature, with vocabulary development and grammar, while improving their writing styles.

One can say that I get a break, since I've got planning third block. Sure, I've got the experience and knowledge, but to teach seventh-grade academics to both math and language arts classes? Our principal seemed to even grin trying

Peggy Kohlmeyer

to compliment me during our preplanning at the beginning of the school year: "I'm sure you can do this!" Yet she still hasn't put her foot in my classroom.

In our kitchen, I open the bottom refrigerator drawer. I'm glad that fixing dinner tonight is going to be easier than I thought. Spinach is in a bag and already washed. Celery, a little green pepper, mushroom, and tomato, adding them all to my bowl. Onion I've previously sliced and in a bag, too. Chicken in the microwave for three minutes, two minutes, one minute, *bing*! It's done. Opening the kitchen drawer, looking for the sharpest knife to cut the chicken, *what would happen if I called in sick tomorrow?* The lights are brightening up; the kitchen light now glints off all our knives. *Would they miss me? Who would cover my classes?* Knowing I have to take the knife out to cut the

Lifelines

microwaved chicken breast for dinner, *what if I didn't call in? What if I didn't show up?* Looking at our knife, the one with the sharpest blade, asking myself *just how sharp is that?* Stepping even deeper into my own dismay and wondering *how bad would it actually hurt to cut my own wrist? Which way do I go? Is it cutting straight down or across?* My mind's darting around. *Mike isn't coming back home for eight more days. How would he know if I didn't call him in the morning? Would he call the school? Would the school call home? Would they tell him that I didn't show up for work? That I didn't call in sick? That I didn't leave a note. No, it's not just a note that I need to write but a letter, a letter to Ms. Smith, my principal. Does she know what she's done? Daily I try and reach those kids. Daily I'm there, but I feel like I am only an eyesore since everyone else has someone else to teach or*

Peggy Kohlmeyer

collaborate with. It's not my fault that the other

school opened and took half our staff and students.

Why did she have to pick me? Yes, a thank-you note

to Ms. Smith for how she has overwhelmed me and

the tension and stresses that I face every single day.

Thinking more, w*ho would clean up the kitchen*

floor? Mike? I can't ask him to come home to that.

Glancing at the kitchen knife again, I quietly close the drawer. Opening the microwave, I put the cooked chicken breast in the refrigerator even though I don't think I'll ever eat it. I would actually have to hold the knife in my hand. Dinner tonight cannot be a threat. I settle for a peanut butter sandwich instead.

The next day, I call. "It's not so much that I need counseling but someone to talk to. Yes, someone to listen to me and give me feedback. Tuesday? After school? Five-thirty? Perfect."

Lifelines

"Carol, thanks for seeing me. I'm not sure what's up, but I've had some dark thoughts, and I don't like them."

"That's what I'm here for, Peggy. What do you mean by dark thoughts?"

"That's only what I call it. I mean, I was in the kitchen, and the light was hurting my eyes. When I turned the light on, it's like a chain of events. One thought led to another that led to another."

"A light?"

"Yes, you know, the normal kitchen fluorescent light. I tried to cover or shield my eyes. I'm thinking if I can block the light out, I won't think the thoughts, only I had to eat. I had to fix dinner."

"Did you have to have this light on?"

Peggy Kohlmeyer

"Yes, pretty much. If the light isn't on, you can't see since we have so many trees in the backyard. They're great in the summer for all their shade, but in the winter, it's totally gloomy."

"What's your reason again for being in your kitchen at this time?"

"Dinner. I even turned leaving the kitchen, but I knew I had to eat. I teach, and if I skip a meal, I don't have any energy."

"Hmm, go ahead."

"I was fixing a spinach salad with chicken. My salad was done, but I couldn't pick up the knife to cut the kitchen. I was too scared. I only thought of the mess that I would make for my husband to clean up when he got home."

"That does seem like a dark thought. I see what you mean. Peggy, where do you work?"

Lifelines

"For the school system. I only have to drive three miles to school. You're also so convenient. I live on the other side of the business park."

"How long have you been there?"

"I've been teaching for nineteen years, but thirteen years now at this school."

"Nineteen years? That's great. I guess you like it?"

"Oh yes, I love it. I mean, I love it when I'm in the class. Seeing the students make the connection with all the effort that I've put forth. That's my reward or rather, I would think every teacher's reward. I work so hard for them. Everything I do every day in some way is for them. It's just takes all my time. I'm there at school at six-thirty or seven o'clock in the morning, and the school day starts at eight-thirty. Don't get me wrong. It's not only in my class that I work, but

Peggy Kohlmeyer

the mornings are also for parent conferences, our weekly faculty meeting, and department meetings. I also tutor every Tuesday. I have to get there before the school day actually starts. After school the kids leave at three-thirty, and after bus duty, I try to leave by four-thirty but to not have a headache or work to do the next morning, I usually stay until five o'clock."

"Hearing what you just said about your school or work, what do you do for *you*?"

"I mean, I do have some time. I go to the gym two times a week and have a trainer, Bear, who totally kicks my butt since he is constantly raising the bar for me to accomplish something new and more challenging. That's my saving grace. It's a complete outlet for me. If it's a great week, I run four times, but it's usually three, but in reality, lately it's only once or twice, and when the chance

Lifelines

is right, meeting my friend Melissa, Melissa
Caldwell."

"With your husband away at work, how do
you spend your weekends?"

"Weekends? Saturday or Sunday? I have to
get set for the upcoming week, and that's five or six
hours. I make all the digital presentations at home
for the kids to see. I also make the master sets to
copy. That's my planning time."

"Peggy, why do you do so much? I
counsel other teachers, and your workload is a
little extreme."

"It is. I'm here since I didn't pick up the
knife. I knew I couldn't trust myself with it. Instead I
had a peanut butter sandwich."

"Did that work for you? I mean, having
the sandwich for dinner?"

Peggy Kohlmeyer

"Yes, but it's also what I took for lunch that day."

"You didn't trust yourself picking up the knife. What made you change your mind?"

"Weirdly enough, my guilt set in, since I hadn't written my principal a letter expressing my thoughts, telling her of the stress that I'm going through to meet the goals that I've set. To meet her goals since she "knows that I can do it." Looking at Carol's puzzled face, I explain, "I teach two classes of math to two different classes of students, which is totally fine, but the first class I see *again* to teach honors language arts. English is my area of love, but the two together? To the same students? "

"Oh, how do you do that? This is also to the middle grades?"

Lifelines

"Yes, seventh grade, the twelve- to thirteen-year-olds. I don't know either sometimes. I just do. I mean, I have the background and degrees for each, but to teach them both at the same time is difficult."

"Your husband, Mike, he's away at work? How does he support you in this?"

"Gosh, when he is home, he is my savior, my escape. When he's gone, I work harder to maybe cover up his absence. When he's not there— at home, I mean—I feel so guilty."

"*Guilty*? Peggy, what do you feel guilty about?"

"Well, that I'm here. I mean that I'm alive."

"What do you mean by this?"

"I'm not sure what I'm here for, why I'm even alive. I was hit a while ago, it was a drunk

Peggy Kohlmeyer

driver, and he hit me head on, and put me in the hospital for three months and a coma."

"Gosh, Peggy, I never would've known. You're doing so much. You've done so much."

"I guess that's it. I've tried to make up for whatever I might have missed. To meet the expectations of my dad. And then the second time was on the exact same road, but in the morning. The girl bumped me while I was in the turning lane. I chased her down. I wasn't in the car by myself, either. I was visiting my mom and grandmother both in Athens."

"The third time, I was running, and the guy was making a right-hand turn. It was in the morning, too. He wasn't drunk. He just didn't pay attention to me as I was following the crossing walk sign, and it blinked for me to go. He didn't turn to see me standing there until he hit me. I mean, his car hit me."

"Peg that sounds like it was pretty bad."

"He only ran over my foot."

"Your foot? Did he break it? Did he break anything? I mean, were you injured?"

"He pulled over and asked if I was OK, but I just wanted to get home…so I ran back to my apartment."

"You ran back home?"

"Yes, I was out for a run, but I did call my mom when I got back. She said I was crazy. She told me to elevate my foot, put ice on it, and go have it X-rayed."

"What did the doctor say when you had it X-rayed?"

"I didn't. I iced it and elevated it, but I had school the next day."

Peggy Kohlmeyer

"Oh. And the fourth time?"

"I was coming home from school on a Tuesday. This guy ran the red light and T-boned my car. After my first car accident, that one was the worst. My jaw was broken before, and here dislocated. Now I've got to wear a bite plate every night."

"But why do you feel guilty? After all that, you're here. You're teaching."

"Yes, but I feel guilty that I haven't met my dad's expectations. I mean, maybe my own expectations."

"Let's start there. I'm going to say this, and yes, you've probably heard it, or as an English teacher, you might have even assigned it," Carol expresses, as I'm almost holding my breath, waiting for her magic answer. "Write it down."

Lifelines

That's it? Of course, I've assigned this. For any good thought, for the clarity of any subject, write it down. What does she want me to write down, though?

"Write down what's bothering you. Write down what you're thinking. Write down those thoughts that we have, that we think and wonder about, write them down."

"Write them down?" To share with her? An essay, a formal letter?

Politely shaking her head no, instead she says, "A little odd asking an English teacher, but do you need some prompts to get started? They're your thoughts. I won't read them, but I want you to address these prompts." She hands me a list of general topics for our next meeting.

"Where do I start? I mean, how do I begin?"

Peggy Kohlmeyer

"Peg, that's not at all what I want you to worry about. I only want you to write."

There is so much that I do not know, memories I seem to have lost. This is a test for me; what I can remember. Mom, Dad, Athens, school, long hot summers, Katie, and having my palm read as a kid.

Chapter 18
Have My Palm Read Again?

After many months of writing down my thoughts, I have a clearer picture of my life, and those memories that I can remember are coming back together. All of these I appreciate and want to share with Mike. Visiting one location that I can recall is the main thoroughfare in downtown Athens, Georgia, or East Broad Street. In its heyday, the downtown area had the expansive storefront windows of Belk's, JC Penney, and Davison's that displayed the trends for the upcoming season.

With the opening of malls—Georgia Square Mall for Athens—the shopping venues of these major department stores have deserted this stretch. As in many other cities in the United States today, a transformation has taken place here. Today's

Peggy Kohlmeyer

downtown Athens is still the hub of the local community while it caters to a different, maybe even eclectic crowd with small boutiques and eateries, which is the reason for our visit.

Walking down East Broad Street, looking around, I'm trying to remember anything specifically that happened to me here. Glancing around with hope, I'm guiding my mind to something that sticks out, something that catches my attention as a flickering thought. But far too many times, I don't know the recall or connection to fill in all the vacant spaces that sometimes occupy my brain. These spaces or holes that I have resemble the holes found in a piece of sliced Swiss cheese. These empty spaces representing the void of the memories that I had as a child.

Looking around before opening the restaurant's front door, I can only take a deep breath, waiting for any possible recall of my childhood

Lifelines

memories to elapse. I'm reminded of the Davison's department store's majestic aura as we enter the swinging double glass doors. The marbled floor entrance still represents a lingering memory with the name *Davison's* scripted in gold letters across it. Releasing my disappointed sigh while searching for some type of childhood connection, I only acknowledge time has definitely passed. A dull lull now replaces the store's original glistening shine that once offered the customer's reflection. Moving farther inside the old building, my eyes are still automatically drawn up to the sprawling chandelier. As my vision floats back down, my eyes rest on the mezzanine. The infamous mezzanine, with the balcony that looks out onto the bottom or first floor, where we stand. Wait, a thought. Now I remember. This is the store where I first tested my independence from Mom.

Peggy Kohlmeyer

Looking to the rear of the first floor, the expansive wooden spiral staircase is still strategically located and intact. I remember this is it. This is where my sprints begin. With me in the first grade, my accomplishment is beating Mom to our agreed-upon point, which is greeting her at the elevator door up there, up on the mezzanine floor. Here, Mom and I check with each other to make sure the other doesn't get lost. The next step is racing to the top or the second floor. With me taking the wooden staircase, I can only speed walk to follow the No Running signs posted. Reaching the second floor as the golden Davison's elevator doors open, I stand holding my breath. Did I make it? Did I beat her?

Grinning with this memory I've just reclaimed, I'm refocusing back to today. The Davison's building still stands tall, but it's now subdivided, leasing to more than one tenant. Walking

Lifelines

through the same swinging front doors as I did so often with Mom, directly on the left is a new restaurant instead of the Davison's men's department. Suddenly, my mind is engulfed with an enormous sudden rush of memories taking up my mind as the dinner table chatter swarms around me.

"What do you want to do next? Since it's only seven o'clock?" Mom's asking, as we've finished our pizza. Gosh I, thought the only dilemma was to find a parking spot. Parking tonight was a similar nightmare. Only this time, due to students out for a pub crawl instead of shoppers trying to get into their favorite department store. Mom's asking me to make the decision of what's up next.

"Mom, what do you usually do on a Friday night?"

"Oh, coffee with Ginny and Sue."

Peggy Kohlmeyer

Acting as my husband Mike's Magellan and guiding him to take the left onto Lumpkin Street through the Five Points traffic light, we make it to Mom's Friday night destination.

Walking into Jittery Joe's Coffee Shop, a quick feeling of uneasiness envelops me. I'm not sure why. Sue and Ginny are only my Mom's friends, but it's been five years. Ten years? No, twenty-five years since I've seen my mom's two closest friends? Wait, over twenty-five years! "Hey, Susan," I'm hearing them both share in unison, greeting my Mom by her first name.

"Hey, Sue; hey, Ginny. We were driving by after dinner and thought we would come in."

"Gosh, Peggy, is that you? My goodness, just look how tall you are. How many years?"

Easily, I recognize Sue Stephenson's voice as if she's calling out to me, back when we were all on

Hope Avenue. Gosh, with time passing and their friendships enduring, I'm back to my childhood years.

"Mrs. Stephenson, Dr. Burg, hi, and this is my husband, Mike."

"Wow, glad to meet you, Mike. Peg, what finally brings you back to Athens?"

My defenses relax with Mrs. Stephenson calling me by that name, with her recognizing me once again as Mom's daughter.

"Since Mom's moving back into our old house, we're using it as an excuse for a quick visit to the Barrow Elementary school festival tomorrow and to run in their 5K race."

"A 5K race? Gosh, with that distance what time do you have to get started?"

"Oh, it's a late race at nine o'clock a.m., which is great since it's been so cold. With the school festival picking up as runners cross the finish line."

"Distance? That's nothing for Peg here. She uses that for her warm-up," Mike heartily chimes in.

"Oh, Mike, stop it. You're giving them the wrong impression. I'm trying to keep up with you!"

"Well, let's slide over here, and you'll take a seat," Ginny Burg warmly extends. Always respectfully addressed as Mrs. Stephenson and Dr. Burg, each one is still the same individual that they were twenty-five years ago, holding and maintaining their friendship with a distinct pecking order. Sue Stephenson, or Mrs. Stephenson for me, always holds the charge of the conversation, supported by Dr. Ginny Burg, followed by Mom. If a new topic is up for discussion, Mrs. Stephenson leads the conversation and tonight that topic happens to be me.

"Peg, this can't be your first visit back to town. Give us some details and catch us up."

"Oh, I've just been teaching in Huntersville."

Lifelines

"How did you do it? I mean, when I saw you at the hospital, the only thought I had was of you pulling through the day. I mean, sorry Peg, but it was heart wrenching to see you."

"Gosh, Mrs. Stephenson, I never knew you were there."

"Peg, remember, I'm the one who had to call your mom since your grandfather Poder had died. She needed to know before she came home. Your grandmother wasn't going to tell her. Your Mimi wasn't in any position since she had to deal with so much herself with your grandfather's death."

"I thought Katie would've told Mom on the way back from the airport. I mean, why didn't she pick Mom up? It was Mom's return trip, back home for the summer from Africa, right?"

"Peg, Katie didn't leave your side or your dad's."

Peggy Kohlmeyer

"Nope, your mom called me from the airport to tell me her plane had arrived from the London connection. I told her that it was your Mimi and Aunt Francis who would pick her up."

"Mom, you didn't know where I was? You didn't know I was at Saint Mary's and what had happened to me?"

"No, Peg, it wasn't until we reached the city of Commerce that Mimi told me that we were going to Saint Mary's."

"Oh, Mom, I'm so sorry. I just took it for granted that since I didn't pick you up in Atlanta, you would've known that something was wrong."

"Peg, it's not your fault. Since Poder had just passed away, I figured this was your grandmother's way of consoling me, picking me up since your grandfather had already been buried."

Lifelines

"Mom, I didn't know. I guess I was pretty bad off. I mean, I don't know," opening up a topic of frightful memories I've barricaded for more than two decades. Mom's response is shared with a grimacing expression enveloping her face. Without a word from her and me reading her body language, she's answered my question.

Looking at Mike and easing my hand into his, "I'm sorry, I didn't know all this." Signifying his support, he simply squeezes my palm.

"Mrs. Stephenson, what actually happened? I just got tired of being the go-between for Katie and Mom. Why doesn't Katie ever just contact Mom herself?"

"You didn't know? No, you don't know, but then everyone took it for granted that you would've found out."

Peggy Kohlmeyer

Asking Mrs. Stephenson, "What do you mean? Why don't they talk? What did she do? What did Katie do?"

"Think of the situation. You were in a coma, and your dad was flying down to Columbus and back every day. Your father stated that he wanted you moved to Saint Francis to know the hospital, the staff, and the doctor in charge."

Dr. Burg continues, "Your mom comes home. Finds the condition that you're in and doesn't want you moved. After such a horrific accident and you still in a coma, who would've thought?"

Following the circle of conversation, I look toward Mom, since it's her turn, instead she glances down toward her coffee cup.

Lifelines

Picking up with Mrs. Stephenson again. "That's when your mom or Mimi took your father to court."

"Custody rights. That's the legal angle. The fight or battle for custody rights, while you're still in a coma." Dr. Burg takes her turn. Coming back to Mom, "I did get to see you for some time. Some more time before you were moved."

I'm totally taken aback with the information of this event. A major life event that involved me. Still puzzled, "So why is it that Katie and Mom…" apologetically looking at my mom, since she's present and sitting right beside me and I'm referring to her "…don't talk?"

"When she testified, Katie stated that your mom left you. Katie stated she left the two of you and went to Africa."

"The law labels this as desertion or child abandonment."

Child abandonment? Deserted us? Which I totally don't understand. "How is Mom supposed to have deserted us? Katie's the reason we went to live with Daddy. Katie's the reason that Mom went to Africa. Mom didn't desert us. Mom left two years after we were already living with Daddy. Katie was back in Athens at the University of Georgia in the same town and never even got in touch with Mom. I'm saying not even a visit. I mean, not even a phone call."

Bringing the situation into light again, Dr. Burg responds, "Peg, who else was there to testify for your mom? Your custodial rights were granted for your benefit. There was nothing that you could say. You were in a coma."

Lifelines

"That's why Katie won't talk to *me*? Is this the same reason that Daddy's distanced himself from me also?"

"Peg, how long has it been?"

"Gosh, for Katie, let's make it ten years. With Daddy the last time was only a drop-by hello from me, when I drove down to Columbus and had a place to stay with my friend Susanne."

"And how long ago was that?"

"Five, six, seven years? Yes, it's been seven years."

"Peg, you can't say you haven't tried, but now you know the reason for their distance, their separation. Even more, after your traumatic event, how have you been? Who have you been speaking to?"

Refocusing my uneasy thoughts back to our conversation, keying in on Mrs. Stephenson's last

Peggy Kohlmeyer

phrase, "after your traumatic event," suddenly I'm in question of myself. What? Me? I went through that?

"Me and a traumatic event?" I direct this to Mrs. Stephenson. "I've always felt that it's only been an obstacle in my life. I mean, everyone has them. I've used it in an analogy to some of my students at school. We all have hurdles in life, and the older we get, sometimes the bigger they become. I follow up with the kids and ask them, 'Is it the hurdle that takes you, or do you take the hurdle and move on?' Why would I need to talk to someone? Someone like who?"

Hearing this from her and having Mrs. Stephenson listen and me sharing, I'm now going into her area of expertise with her professional response as a psychologist. "A counselor, someone in the special area of trauma."

Lifelines

With her saying this out loud, I'm totally puzzled.

Trauma? How does what happened to me more than twenty-five years ago even qualify as trauma? I'm not making this connection. "Doesn't everyone have the experiences or hurdles that I've had, but just in a different form?"

"Peg, realize what's happened to you isn't the norm," with the conversation rotating to Dr. Burg now taking the speaker's seat. "Getting updates from your mom, looking at you, and the hurdles, as you've called them, you've definitely overcome them, but think of what's missing. That's the part that could be holding you back."

"What's missing for you in completing tomorrow's race?"

With her statement, I've connected to the emptiness that I've had. All my past experiences that I can't even recall. Responding in my own defense, "I say that my mind isn't blank, just full of holes where my memories used to be."

"That's what I am referring to; seeing a psychologist, a counselor will help you take away the block that you've put up for many of the experiences that you've had here. Simply enough, just help yourself and write them down." Her statement is my reinforcement of what Carol in Huntersville also asked me to do.

Jarring me back to today, Dr. Burg reminds us it's February, and it is wintertime. "The forecast is twenty-three degrees tomorrow morning."

Looking around the Jittery Joe's table, I'm reminded where I am and that I'm sharing time with people who care about me: Mike, my mom, Mrs. Stephenson, and Dr. Burg.

Lifelines

"Gosh, Mom, I'm so sorry. We're here to meet with your friends, and I've hogged your conversation." Looking over at Mike to include him, too. "Mike, I'm so sorry."

Mike having his perfect timing as to when to step in: "Peg, Mrs. Pike, look at the time. We're going to need to leave and get back to the house with us getting up for that run tomorrow."

In my old bedroom back at Mom's house, setting out our running clothes to prepare for tomorrow's race, "Mike, I just didn't know. Katie made a huge scrapbook for me. Looking through it, she begins it with newspaper articles of the accident. It's got all the cards from flowers that people sent and get-well letters, too, but at the end, it's all about Mom and Dad going to court. I mean, I've seen it, I've read

Peggy Kohlmeyer

it. It's about me, but I've never made any real connection to it, like it's really me."

"Peg, did you ever ask yourself what if your Mom had won? I mean, what if she had gotten custody, and you stayed in Athens? With her working overseas, how long would that have been? Basically, how would you be the same? I think your sister, Katie, actually did you a favor. She knew then what was best for you, and that's what she told the judge."

"Mike, now I'm feeling bad. Maybe Katie's always has done the best for me. Only I didn't know."

Barrow Elementary School still gives me that warm inside glow as Mike and I walk into the newly added gym for our race. Picking up our numbers with the fanfare of the booth displays for the carnival adds that additional excitement. As with everyone who goes back to a place as an adult, everything seems so much smaller now.

Waiting for the start of the race in the front of the school building, looking up at Mike. "This is it. This is where Mrs. Aldridge, my first-grade teacher, had all of us outline our bodies on a huge sheet of paper and write what we wanted to be when we grew up."

"What did yours say? A runner, a teacher, or a kid at heart who never grows up?"

"No, a ballet dancer!"

"What? You wanted to be a ballet dancer when you grew up? Where did you get that one from?"

"Come on, Mike, yes, a ballet dancer. I wanted to be a ballet dancer because my friend Missy wanted to be a teacher, and I couldn't be the same thing she wanted to be, so I picked something that she couldn't become since she didn't go and take lessons. A ballet dancer."

"How did you get that one? I mean, you're five feet ten. How did you ever come up with that one? There aren't any dancers that tall."

"But this was in first grade, and I wasn't that tall." Gosh, that thought just came out. I have no idea where it came from. I'm remembering standing next to my new friend Missy and making silhouettes of each another and our posters and writing our paragraphs about growing up. "Mike, I think this is going to be a great race."

"*Runners lining up at the starting line!*"

"And the carnival afterward?"

"Mike, let's skip that if you don't mind…Skip the temptation of having our life lines read by the palm reader."

Lifelines

"What? Why? That would be fun. Skip it? I don't understand. Don't you want to know?"

"*Runners on your mark…*"

"Want to know? Oh, Mike, after we finish this race, I'll tell you what I can without having my palm read again."

Peggy Kohlmeyer

Chapter 19
An Interesting Invitation

For most people, time passes by the second; the minute; the hour; the day; and of course, the month and year. With me, time passes by class periods, days of the week, grading cycles of either weeks in a quarter or semester, and then the school year. When I speak of a year it's not the calendar year of January to December, but the school year from August to June. When January rolls around, it's not the beginning of the new year, but halfway through the school year with the ending of the first semester. With many years as a teacher, isn't this how all teachers operate?

Another Monday after school and I'm at the Huntersville Family Fitness and Aquatics Center or my local gym. After talking to middle schoolers for the day, adult conversation is needed even if it's a passing, "How many more sets?" to the fellow member on whatever exercise machine. Hearing someone politely mention my name, "Peg, hey, Peg," I see a fellow gym member. It's Tim, who adds, "We're having an open adult fellowship program. Would you be interested in speaking?"

I'm thrown a little off my path, since I'm at the gym to work out my body, and someone is asking me to tap into my brain. My only response to him is "What?" allowing me time to focus on what he's asking, while also implying with my question that I need some more information for his invitation.

"For the month of January, instead of the traditional Sunday school classes, all the adults are meeting in the fellowship hall as one group. Every week we're having a guest speaker, and you'd be a perfect fit. You could share your event. Don't worry, I mean, you don't have to have a direct link to God.

Lifelines

Our organizer will do that. You'll just share your experience."

"Speak in front of adults?" Every weekday, I speak to my seventh-grade students when I teach, but in front of actual adults? That is definitely a different audience. "How many people, Tim?"

"Only about twenty."

That's not too big or too small, compared to my usual class size around thirty. "For how long?"

"About twenty minutes. That'll give ten or fifteen minutes for questions and answers afterward."

Hmm, I'm contemplating to myself. Tim's asking me to speak for twenty minutes in front of adults about myself. Gosh, why would anyone ever be interested in me? What story is he speaking about? "Interested? Just give Donna a call at the Huntersville Church for the details."

Share my event? He must be talking about my car accident. My mishap. Me being at the wrong place at the wrong time. I'm making the connection that Tim read about me in the newspaper article in the *Lake Norman News* this week. When someone says it's a small world, this pretty much is the label for Huntersville. Having known the faces at the Huntersville Family Fitness and Aquatics Center for eleven or twelve years, Tim Landry's face is familiar, and to speak at his church, it's something for me to consider.

Thinking back to the week before, having an article about myself in the newspaper was *not* the reason I stopped Jim Deem at the grocery story. In fact, I'm thinking about the upcoming writing unit of personal narratives for school. Having Jim Deem

Lifelines

return as a guest lecturer could only benefit my students again this year. Since I had previously taught Jim Deem's daughter in my English class, Jim had been a guest speaker last year, addressing my students on the reason to write and answering the question "Why?" Why is it that someone even needs to take the time to read what you have written?

Picking up on the coincidence of seeing Jim, and before expressing my returning invitation for him to speak to my students again, I simply questioned him. "What are you working on now?" With my one question to him, I did it, I spilled the beans, or my beans, about my personal connection to a drunk driver experience that had just occurred in town.

Respecting him for his profession and what Mr. Deem had published regarding a drunk driving teen, I told him my side. The opposite side. Jim's article that I'm speaking about told of the teen who

Peggy Kohlmeyer

was the driver and was drunk, and she hit a man head on, placing him in the hospital, and her life now after the accident. It was the opposite of my story, since I was the one who had been hit and lived. This resulted in last week's article that Mr. Deem wrote about me as the living, breathing, standing opposite event following his previous article. It had to be the article that Tim from the gym was referring, or my side of the story. I hadn't mentioned it to anyone like this *ever*. I felt that it had been my own secret. With Tim Landry asking me to speak at his church and trusting him for this invitation, I'll follow through and give Donna at the church a call as he invited.

Whether it's seventh graders during the school week or adults on a Sunday, the key to a good presentation is capturing the audience and keeping *their* interest. What's going to capture their attention? What's something that I can express and display, so they can make a connection? *Hmmm*, pictures, pictures, pictures and maybe even X-rays.

My scheduled date of January 21 arrives, and shaking from the winter chill, I begin addressing the Sunday audience with the formal greeting, "Good morning, ladies and gentlemen." Looking back to the doorways, there are more than the twenty or twenty-five people Tim had suggested. This room is packed with people standing in the back, and all the folding chairs taken.

It's a sweater dress I'm wearing for this morning's season and weather, but now I'm starting to sweat. At least I picked out a dark knit, so no one can easily see my perspiration marks. I'm quickly called back to this morning's event with the "Good morning" in unison from the audience, in response to my initial introduction.

Peggy Kohlmeyer

"With the invitation from your fellow church member, Tim Landry," nodding my head in acknowledgment to him and his wife, "I'm using this time to share a deeply personal major life experience with you." As I'm trying not to allow my voice to tremble, expressing my sudden fear of sharing my story. "As a seventh-grade English teacher, I'm thanking you ahead of time, with you as my first audience. At my school, we begin our next unit with the personal narrative. Let me know how my presentation plays out, and if it's good enough information to also grab my students' attention next week." Hearing a few audience chuckles, I'm quickly eased to continue.

"Right now, take a moment. I'm asking you if you receive the *Lake Norman News*? Last week's article about the intoxicated teen who hit the man." Giving them a few moments to ponder, I see the

Lifelines

similar look that my students in class have when I've asked them to think or reflect. Their eyes go up and start to shift, meaning they're making some connection.

"Raise your hand if you've read it. Who can share what they thought?" One, two, three hands are up...Good, I'm getting that audience participation. "Yes, you, ma'am?"

"As a mom, I felt sorry for the family of the teen and what she did."

"You, sir?"

"I guess I'm the opposite, I feel sorry for the man who was hit and his family."

Now stepping in to address both: "I take it that's how we would naturally feel, sorry for one side or the other. In the *Lake Norman News* this week, Mr. Deem, shared my story. The other side of a similar story, although...I'm the one who got hit.

Peggy Kohlmeyer

Now giving a pause for people to think, I'm pointing up to the large projector screen. "Looking at the screen, I've listed some numbers. Not that I'm classified as a numerologist, but I really like how numbers don't lie. I've used these numbers to represent the events in my life." I read them off the screen:

0, 1, 3, 4, 14, 17, 24, 25, 32, 87, 2500, 17024

"Starting at the left, the number that isn't a number is actually an empty value, zero. This is actually a number I could end with, since it's the amount of money I didn't receive from a lawsuit. The driver who hit me had just been released from jail that day. It was his fourth arrest while driving intoxicated, or DWI. Again, that zero there is what I received from a lawsuit that didn't go through. Yes, he killed himself." Hearing the gasps and a few *Oh*s from the audience, I pause for a moment. "From what I was told, he wrote his wife a letter or note, stating that he couldn't go back to jail knowing his sentence could only be longer, and not having the alcohol he so depended on, he shot himself.

"Who here can share a connection that they have to the number one? Yes, sir?"

"The number of children in our family right now." Glancing to his wife, who is pregnant with their second child.

With subtle laughter from the crowd responding to him, "Thank you and congratulations, sir, and after two, maybe number three?" He's grinning while his pregnant wife only sighs deeply. "Who else would like to share? Yes, ma'am?"

"One cigarette, that's my goal today." Applause came from the audience to demonstrate their support. "That's great, a good beginning to stop smoking." Pulling the audience's attention back to me. "Following the zero, that number one for me is the number of marathons that I've done." Hearing their applause for this 26.2-mile run, I quickly respond, "Thank you, but no, my love for running isn't what I'm trying to achieve or prove with that number as my first, but keeping that number in mind, my reason will come to you later.

"Looking at the numbers again, number 3 is the number that follows, representing the number of months that I lost after this drunk driver hit me head on. I'd been in the hospital for three months. My months of June, July, and August were gone. Leaving the hospital where my father worked wasn't new, so I didn't question leaving Saint Francis Hospital. Three months later, leaving the hospital, I still did *not know* something had happened. I just thought it was another visit to see my dad.

Lifelines

"Looking at the numbers again, number 4 follows. This shows my love for running. I've done four half marathons. Followed by number 5, representing the number of my teeth that were *not* lost or damaged after getting hit head-on." Now I'm pointing to my dental X-ray, which shows the hollow areas for my teeth that have been permanently replaced.

Looking forward, facing the audience, I continue. "With medical terminology, a coma is a concussion and is a bruise to the brain, which induces a coma. Boy, did I have a bruise. Fourteen days with this type of bruise, or in a coma, doesn't allow one to wake up and say, "Oh, my gosh, what happened?" That's why the number fourteen jumps ahead and is next. I was in a coma for fourteen days.

"With every individual, every accident, and every person's body, the healing process is different.

Peggy Kohlmeyer

Connecting with reality for me at that time wasn't permanent. A huge gray fog enveloped me at times. I was the definition of clueless. My mind comparable to a slice of Swiss cheese with holes or empty spaces that needed to be refilled. My first trip leaving my dad's house was back to the hospital to remove the pins or tacks from my gum that allowed my jaw to be wired together. My second trip out of the house was another return to the hospital.

This time, it was to rebreak my right leg to have it properly reset. It had not been set properly, and my tibia and fibula now overlapped, resulting in it being one and a half inches shorter than my left one. This was a wasted trip, since my bones were already fused, and it would have required extensive corrective surgery due to their length discrepancy.

"On our third trip, it was a bit different. This time, we dropped in to visit one of my dad's friends.

Lifelines

By friend I mean doctor friend, at his doctor's office. With my father's presence for each previous visit and me pretty much clueless on the trips to the hospital, it wasn't until I heard the sound of a saw in this friend's office that I quickly realized something *had* happened to me. Hearing the sound of a saw in the office of my orthopedist snaps me back to full reality. My father, seeing my expression of complete fear, now understood that I didn't know what's going on.

"Dr. Johnson approached me and seeing him press the electric saw onto my left cast at my knee, I was thinking he was going to cut my leg off. I mean, what else do you do with a hand-held electric saw? Ladies and gentlemen, I didn't know how to react.

"Again, I saw Dr. Johnson pressing this hand-held chainsaw against my cast. Deliberately, he was moving it slowly from my knee to my toe. I asked myself, what did I do to deserve this? Clenching my hands, waiting to see my own blood spurt out with his first cut.

"Finishing, lifting, and turning the saw off, Dr. Johnson pried open the edges he made along my cast. Ladies, I hadn't been able to shave my leg in three months. Looking down at my own leg, I only see a gorilla-haired shin that doesn't even belong to me. This is a complete out-of-body experience. Mentally, I'm not grasping that it's my calf there. It's been covered up by the plaster, and I haven't been able to see it, making it not there for me.

"Today I understand, right at this point in time, my mind is making the connecting to object permanence. In a child's mind this is a step takes place between two and three years old. When the cover of an object is removed, the object is actually there. Here, right here, just previously, my own cognition wasn't grasping this concept for me with my head trauma." Hearing the heartfelt sighs released from the parents, knowing of their own kids and development.

"Releasing my grip on the examination table and needing a good jolt of positive information, I gathered the gumption to ask Dr. Johnson, 'What are my chances of running in the Peachtree Road Race next year?' Not addressing me or acknowledging that I've even asked him a question, Dr. Johnson only went on with what he was doing. Next, he gently placed one of his hands on the side of my foot, as if to hold it, and with his other hand, he placed his fingers on a metal tab. This, I later realized. was a pin.

"He began to pull this pin. The sensation hit me. I was feeling something, but I wasn't sure what it was. My mind wasn't making the connection for this pain. I was feeling it in my brain, but I didn't know where it was coming from, which was this pin that he was pulling out of my foot.

"Quickly, I was smelling a strong, rotten scent as he was pulling and removing this pin. Here I realized I was smelling my own rotten flesh. This pin set the seventeen breaks in my left foot.

"Pain? I asked myself, 'Is this pain? A pain that I'd never consciously felt before he pulled that pin out?' Right then, my body was in such a shock, I couldn't even scream. I knew it was my pain, but mentally I couldn't make the connection that it was me, and it was from the pin he pulled out of my foot. Without hesitation, he again placed a hand on the top of my foot, holding my toes, while grasping the second pin. Now I'm making this connection between what he was doing and the pain that I would feel. Wanting to get back for what was happening to

Lifelines

me and the pain he'd caused, I let out my loudest scream that my lungs could give.

"Dr. Johnson, now responding to my question about running the Peachtree Road Race only said, 'Let's just see if you can walk again.' Number 17, which you see next on the screen, is for the seventeen breaks in my left foot." I take a few seconds and a deep breath for the audience to make any possible connections.

"Crying in the car as my dad drove me back home wasn't for the pain, that pain was gone. This time, I was crying for knowing something was wrong with me. I was asking myself *why?* Not asking myself why this happened to me, not having the concept that something had, but *why* did I miss the race, *why* are my friends gone, *why* can't I do more for myself and *why* don't I know more? Did I mention feeling clueless, not connecting to reality? Daily fading in and out? This all leads to me asking myself how many people I've disappointed by the way my life has turned out.

"Looking at the screen once again after the number seventeen, number twenty-four follows. In addition to the seventeen breaks in my left foot, the other breaks that are also listed in Mr. Deem's article include my right leg with that forty-five-degree break. On this X-ray," turning to point the visible difference where the bones overlap, "one can see how the bones slid down and settled on top of one another, which means my right leg is permanently shorter than my left leg." As I expected, a few slight gasps from the congregation.

"A fractured pelvic bone, my fractured right rib, which punctured my right lung, my right collarbone, and my fractured chin." Here, I proceed to the next slide. "which separated going into my brain to put me in the coma. This ring," pointing to my chin, specifically to the metal ring on the dental X-ray, "is what was placed to hold it together. With the upper portion of the left side of my jawbone knocked out, which I feel counts, since cement was used to replace it, this brings the count to twenty-four. This number represents the total number of bones that were broken in my body." Here I refrain from looking at the audience, since I can almost feel their eyes burning into me, trying to see any outside mark where all this happened.

"Number twenty-five is up next." Not to get long winded and lose the audience's attention, I slightly gesture to the next number on the screen. To have them not think about me and my body and breaks, but rather what I'm sharing I question them, "What does this number represent to you? Who would like to share?"

Peggy Kohlmeyer

"Yes, ma'am."

"That's the age I was married."

Smiling and nodding, I go on to another lady. "Yes, ma'am?"

"That's the age of our oldest son."

Not taking sides after asking two women, I see one gentleman, and I say, "Yes sir," calling on him standing in the back.

"That's my current age." A chuckle from the audience and I make the connection that he's the previous woman's son.

Beginning again, I say, "This is the high-school reunion," knowing that I didn't graduate from any high school, but it's too much information to share, "that I'm invited to in my hometown of Athens, Georgia." Now I see people my age and older grin and smile, remembering theirs. "For me this becomes the opposite of celebration, as this is the time that

Lifelines

everything that I have talked about finally comes into focus. Dropping into a deeper voice to mark my emphasis of the timing of this event. "I'm saying that it's taken twenty-five years for me to make the connection that this horrendous event happened to me."

Gasps, whoas and a sorrowful oh no resonate from the church's hall.

"Meeting former classmates and recognizing a few faces. One guy, Ray makes a direct line to greet my husband, Mike, and me. Not the greeting of a hi or a hello, but 'What are you doing here?' is all he asks. Puzzled, my only response is, 'I mean, I was invited and all.' He answers with 'No, no, you failed. You failed, you can't be here! You're supposed to be dead.'" From his comment, I was flabbergasted, and from the look of the audience, they were, too.

Peggy Kohlmeyer

I continue. "Ray says 'I was your EMT with the ambulance from Saint Mary's Hospital that day you had your accident. I saw you. You're supposed to be dead.' I'm puzzled, looking at my husband to confirm he's hearing what I'm hearing. I only reply, 'Ray, therefore I owe you my deepest thanks. I'm alive since you were such a success that day. Thank you.'

"Not knowing if I responded correctly Ray's comment jarred me into a connection with what has fully happened to me. He was there. He's an eyewitness, telling me that I failed. It was me, and now I've got to have the strength to own it and admit to it that *I am a failure* since I didn't die."

Taking a deep breath for myself and allowing the audience to also pause, I point to number thirty-two. "Raise your hand if you know how to swim." Glancing around, making eye contact with as many

Lifelines

people as I can. "This is how it started for me. That one dreaded word that I disliked so much because it meant I had to sweat, *exercise*." A few people, mainly women, chuckle. That's the reaction that I need to ease the audience. "When I was attending the University of Georgia, a guy mentioned that he was interested in me, but he couldn't ask me out since it was summer, and it meant going to the pool, and my thighs were too fat." I hear a few gasps. "Therefore, I did the opposite. I didn't wait on him to ask me to the pool. I went to the pool by myself and swam, and swam, and yes, swam. My gratitude goes to him afterward for that comment.

"When I had my accident, the car's front dashboard and steering wheel slammed into my chest, and I received a fractured right rib that punctured my right lung. My dad told me that my lung had been punctured for three days. Three days breathing on one lung before it was noticed. One could say now I owe that guy. I mean, he did motivate me and with swimming you surely workout your lungs.

"Now, raise your hand if you know how to ride a bike." I'm impressed. Only slightly fewer hands than before. "Simple enough, raise your hand if you run, jog, or walk." Fortunately for me, this isn't a limiting question. Now I'm pointing back to number thirty-two. "For me, that number represents triathlons, thirty-two." Here the audience is more astonished than I thought they would be.

"Don't get me wrong. Not the Ironman by any means, but the sprint distance." Hearing a few sighs, "I figured if I could swim, bike, and run, I would try to put them together to see how I would do. And I did."

Lifelines

Jumping ahead of myself in time and relying on the numbers to keep me in order, I continue with the next number displayed, eighty-seven. "Weighing in at eighty-seven pounds after the accident with the cast on my right leg still on and going up to my hip, I couldn't even walk. Initially, my muscles had atrophied to less than those of a newborn baby. Lift a pencil? A pen? A spoon or a fork? Ladies and gentlemen, simply glancing at a pencil within my reach, I wanted it, and I could see it, but my mind wouldn't make the connection of how to pick it up. Much more, I didn't even have the strength. And with my right collarbone broken when I *was* able to pick it up, I couldn't read what I tried to write. Also, for three months in the hospital, I had depended on a catheter, and I had not yet learned to control my own bladder. And the question that I still ask myself is *why*? Why couldn't I do any of this? What happened to my life? My plan?

"When I got home from the hospital, the best thing ever was an empty house. Having a hospital bed in the bonus room of my father's home put me close enough to the restroom. I saw how close it was, and holding onto the bed rail, touching the sofa, the wall, and then the bathroom door, I achieved my first success getting somewhere by myself.

"As my physical efforts continued to improve, *mentally* I also tried, but any recall of a memory was futile. Now don't get me wrong; if someone prompted me, I knew what to do, but it was embarrassing, making all the mistakes. It was my failure of not having the recall to make this simple connection. Sitting in the dark, knowing the difference between night and day, but not knowing how to turn on a light switch. My sister actually had

Lifelines

to flip it up for me one evening for me to be able to see. I followed suit, and now I have a habit of leaving too many lights in the house on. That hairy leg that I had after three months in a cast? Sure, a razor would take care of that, but holding one in my hand and not knowing what to do or what it was for, my sister initially had to demonstrate. Here I began my *aha* moments.

Yes, my mind was a piece of swiss cheese, but these holes were starting to fill slowly and surely. My own cognition was starting to get back on track, and in my mind, ideas began popping up. What about school? My degree? I only knew my immediate answer was to finish college, to gain some personal worth. I had to go back to school. I had to finish my degree. Connecting to the article, again my question is still why?

Peggy Kohlmeyer

"Skipping over many, many details and a fast-forward to three years later, I earned my undergraduate degree, established my career, and finished my ultimate physical goal of completing the Peachtree Road Race. Three years late, but it's done. For others, my life is back on track, and I should be fulfilled. But I'm not. There's some place in me that still has an empty hole. And I've been patiently waiting for an answer to my *why*?

"No, not for me to ever ask *why* such an accident happened to me, but *why* am I alive? What is my purpose in life now supposed to be? Visiting both hospitals in Athens and Columbus, Georgia, I realized I have so many people to thank for what I'm now able to do. Surely the nurses, the doctors, and the entire medical staff, but what about all the other employees who are needed to have the hospital work? It quickly emerged that my thank-you notes would be too

Lifelines

numerous to even start, and then it dawned on me…I have to teach. I have to give my thanks to those individuals by giving to others, the others being our future of tomorrow, for a better tomorrow. A low estimation of that is twenty-five hundred, or the next number on the screen."

Again, I politely gesture toward it. "This represents the number of students whom I've taught, contributing daily to our community and giving my thanks. Daily I give thanks for my life events. Thankful for such a devastating accident? No, thankful that I can give back to the community and daily answer my own question that Mr. Deem asked my students: *why*?

"Looking at the remaining numbers on the screen, number one-seven-zero-two-four follows," I tell the audience. And pointing up to the number one, I say, "Remember when I said that this is number of the marathons that I've run and to remember that? Well, almost every time I run, for whatever distance or event, I'm reminded of what my orthopedist, Dr. Johnson, said when I asked him if I could do the Peachtree Road Race the following year. His answer to me, 'Let's see if you can walk again,' comes back to my mind. Ladies and gentlemen, seventeen thousand twenty-four is the number of logged or recorded miles that I've run, and I'm still adding to it." Seeing a few mouths drop open and eyes open a little wider, I know I've made some type of impact or example.

"I've found a statement to share that the actress and country singer Reba McEntire is known for. I agree with her when she said, 'To thrive in life you need three bones. A wishbone…'" holding up my index finger for emphasis on the number one, "'…a backbone…'" followed by my middle finger for number two, "'…and a funny bone,'" followed by my ring finger to mark the total, three. Holding my hand up an extra second showing my three fingers for the representation of the three bones, I continue, "I don't ask *why* this accident happened to me or rather for me, since this is a situation of triumph in which numerous times I've called upon those three bones."

Now I drop my hand down to my side. "Ladies and gentlemen, in closing, I do know daily I give thanks for the air that I'm able to breathe, for the footsteps that I'm able to take, and the people I'm able to help. Also, at this time, I give my thanks to you for your time, that you've allowed me to share *my* life events."

Peggy Kohlmeyer

www.ingramcontent.com/pod-product-compliance
Lightning Source LLC
Chambersburg PA
CBHW071244250626

47163CB00002B/313